THE ATONEMENT

AN ARRANGEMENT NOVEL, BOOK THREE

KIERSTEN MODGLIN

Cover Design by Kiersten Modglin
Copy Editing by Three Owls Editing
Proofreading by My Brother's Editor
Formatting by Kiersten Modglin

First Print and Electronic Edition: 2022
kierstenmodglinauthor.com

This one's to Ainsley and Peter.
The characters who changed my life, my career, and who made so many of my dreams come true.
This goodbye is bittersweet, but here's to all we've been through and everything the future holds for us.

AUTHOR'S NOTE

Dear Reader,

Thank you for picking up this book! THE ATONEMENT is the third and final book in my bestselling ARRANGEMENT trilogy. In order to fully understand the events in this book, it's important that you start at the beginning. If you haven't had a chance to read THE ARRANGEMENT, start there: http://mybook.to/arrangement, next check out THE AMENDMENT: mybook.to/theamendment, and then come back here for the conclusion to this dark and scandalous story.

Thanks so much for your support. I hope you love every thrilling moment!

XO,

Kiersten

CHAPTER ONE

AINSLEY

My husband was alive.

He was alive and he shouldn't be.

That was my fault.

I checked the rearview, both for signs of being followed and to make sure my children were still there. Still asleep. Still safe. But for how long?

How long did we have until he found us?

Maybe he already had.

I'd read over his text message what felt like a thousand times, until my eyes blurred with tears, fear, and fury.

Then, I'd loaded up my kids, sand still drying on their damp legs, and we'd rushed back to the hotel. I couldn't tell them what was happening—could never tell them what I'd done, so instead, I said very little. They understood something was very wrong—I never let them see me so distraught—and I was grateful when they moved with me, packing their things quickly and loading them into the rental car without too many questions.

We were coming home from our vacation days early, but the stress I wore like a blinding hazard sign seemed to keep them from complaining.

"Is everything okay?" Maisy had asked once more, after her brothers had both fallen asleep. I wanted to be honest with her, truly I did, but what could I say?

What could I ever tell her in order to make her understand how we got here?

As I stared into the headlights approaching our car on the quiet highway, I had to wonder how exactly we *had* gotten here.

Ten years ago—hell, two years ago even, if someone had told me this was what would become of us, I would've laughed at them. Because it was ridiculous.

We were normal people.

A normal family.

Two loving parents.

Three perfect children.

How, then, had we managed to fall this far so fast?

I knew the answer without having to think about it, really.

Peter.

The answer was always Peter.

He was the reason I'd had to make the choices I did. He was the reason for all my mistakes. No matter what I did, nothing seemed to faze him, nothing seemed to make him want to change...not for me, not for his kids, not for anything.

And now, he was refusing to die.

The easiest thing he could've done, yet he refused.

While I could predict almost everything about him, I had no idea what would be running through my husband's mind at that moment, and that scared me maybe more than anything else.

Being unable to stay one step ahead of him simply because he wasn't meant to have any steps left, had caused me to stumble.

And I'd always prided myself on my ability to *never* stumble.

As the car behind us gained speed, the bright headlights blinding me in the rearview, my stomach lurched.

It couldn't be him.

There was no way.

And yet, every car that passed us, I worried. Every gas station I'd stopped at, I'd scanned the faces of each person I passed, convinced that as I rounded a corner, he'd be there. Waiting for me. Waiting for me with that stupid, charming smile.

Was he going to make me pay for what I did?

Not if I could help it, no.

My children needed me to stay alive. They needed me to protect them—from the world and from their father.

Next to me, Maisy stirred against the cool pane of the window. I checked on the boys again. Dylan's mouth hung open in the back seat, his head resting against his seat belt, and Riley was all but lying down.

They would be hungry soon, I suspected. And ready

for showers. The car was caked with sand at that point, but there was just no time for us to stop. We had to keep moving for as long as we could.

I wasn't sure where we were going or where we would be safe. All I knew was that I couldn't let him find us.

I couldn't let him ever find us again.

I slowed down as the car grew closer, willing it to pass me, to let me know it wasn't following us. Instead, the driver slowed too, still following me closely despite the clear left lane.

Chills lined my arms.

No.

I was overreacting.

Being paranoid.

It wasn't Peter.

Reaching forward, I turned the radio down further, driving with only the hum of the road noise in my ears as I searched for signs and weighed my options.

The likelihood that Peter had found us so quickly was terribly low, but I couldn't put anything past him. How long had he had to track us down, after all? How long had I lain on the beach thinking I'd won, thinking I was finally free, yet all the while I'd failed in every way?

How stupid could I have been?

I should've made sure it was done.

But there was no sense dwelling on the past or hating myself for my mistakes. All there was left to do was fix things. Fix everything.

It's what I was best at, after all.

CHAPTER TWO

AINSLEY

To my relief, the kids managed to sleep through the night, giving me enough time to formulate some semblance of a plan by the time we arrived in Nashville early the next morning.

I couldn't take them home.

Though I suspected Peter was already long gone, I couldn't risk it.

School wasn't an option either, as I'd piggybacked the vacation to start before fall break, but even if I hadn't, I assumed he'd check there.

I crossed Glennon's home off my mental checklist too —she was still out of town, but it would also be another one of the first places Peter would think to look for us.

A hotel was out in case he checked our bank statements, which would've already led him to Florida, and then this direction. I'd taken out cash at every station that would let me, so I could space out my need for using the debit card, but even still, I'd left a trail.

My options were limited. In truth, I could only see one viable choice, and it was an incredibly bitter pill to swallow.

As the sun rose that morning, painting the sky a brilliant shade of purple, I pulled into the driveway of the house I'd spent the last few decades of my life avoiding.

It was the one place he'd never look for us.

When the car rolled to a stop in front of the two-story colonial home, always bright white with deep-red shutters, I gripped one wrist with my opposite hand and squeezed as tightly as I could, bringing pain to the forefront of my mind.

I needed to focus.

This wasn't going to be permanent.

It was only until we could get our bearings.

When the pain had numbed, the exercise no longer working, I released my wrist and cleared my throat, checking my reflection in the mirror. She'd never forgive me for letting myself go so badly.

Despite that fact, I would put up with whatever torture my mother put me through if it meant keeping my children safe.

Maisy was the first to wake, twisting in the passenger seat to stare at me with one eye open. "Mom?" she croaked, seeming to have forgotten where she was. She sat up, looking around. "Why are we at Grandma's?"

I wondered if she'd recognize the place. We'd been there only a handful of times since she was born.

I sighed. "We're going to visit her for the day."

"Why?" Her forehead wrinkled with obvious

concern. Though I'd done my best to never speak ill of either set of the children's grandparents in front of them, I knew they understood things weren't always civil between us.

"It's just for the day. I have some errands to run, and your dad isn't home. I don't want to leave you three by yourselves."

"Why?" She wasn't complaining exactly; she sounded more confused than anything. The kids were old enough to be left alone, I knew, and plenty mature, but that didn't stop me from worrying. Even with the privacy and security our land had afforded us, I'd learned monsters lurk in the most ordinary places.

After Dylan's most recent birthday, we'd been discussing letting him keep his siblings home alone, but it had never been decided.

Now, I guessed the decision rested solely with me.

Though, to be honest, the thought of ever letting them out of my sight at all was agonizing now.

"It's just for the day, okay?"

Her expression smoothed, her voice rising an octave. "Is that what this is about? Did... Was Grandma the one who texted you? Is she sick? Did something happen?"

I put up a hand to calm her nerves, then used it to smooth her hair. "No, no. It's nothing like that."

"What's going on?" Dylan asked, startling us both as he stretched his arms over his head and released a loud yawn.

"Something's wrong with Grandma," Maisy said.

"What? Seriously?" He unbuckled, leaning closer to us.

"No," I said firmly. "Nothing is wrong with your grandmother."

"Then why are we here?" Maisy asked. "Why did we have to end our vacation? Who texted you when we were on the beach?" Her expression was pinched. Serious. Concerned. She would make quite the little lawyer someday, if she wanted to.

"I've told you, it was a work thing. Which is why we're here. I need to run into work this morning, and I need you three to stay with your grandmother."

"Why are you being weird?" Dylan asked plainly.

"Huh?" Riley was awake now too, rubbing sleep from his eyes.

"Look," I said with a long inhale. "I know this is all... really odd. But I need you guys to trust me, okay? Everything's fine. We're all fine. You're going to be fine. I just need to run into work and deal with a few things, and then we'll go."

"Go where? Go home?" Maisy asked.

"Maybe."

"*Maybe?*"

"Probably," I corrected myself. "Now, come on, you all must be starving and ready for showers. Let's get inside and get cleaned up, okay?" Without waiting for their answers, I pushed my door open and stepped out of the car, moving around to the trunk to retrieve our luggage.

Once we each had our bags, we trudged up the long

concrete walkway toward the shadow-filled porch and its black front door. The air was chilly, causing goose bumps to line my arms, and I wished the sky was brighter. I couldn't help worrying about who might be watching us.

I saw Peter everywhere—in the shapes of the trees across the lawn, behind the columns as we neared them. I couldn't tell my children this, though, so instead, I moved forward without a shred of hesitation. They needed to believe every lie I was selling them.

Every lie I was trying desperately to sell myself.

When we'd reached the door, I pressed a finger into the doorbell. It was just after six in the morning, which meant my mother should be awake, though probably not expecting company. I should've called, I supposed, but that would give her the chance to turn us away, and I couldn't risk that.

After a few moments' pause, I pressed a finger into the doorbell again and gave the kids an encouraging nod.

"Happy faces," I reminded them. "It's early. Let's all be friendly, okay?"

Several awkward minutes passed, giving me just enough time to begin second-guessing my decision, before the door swung open and my mother stood in front of us. Her graying-brown hair was pulled back in a soft headband that matched the white robe she'd tied around herself. She looked left, then right, as if she couldn't see us, then eyed me.

"Ainsley? What in the world are you doing here?" She studied the children. "Is everything alright?"

"Everything's fine," I assured her. "We came for a visit."

"*A visit?*" She said it as if I'd suggested we'd come for the royal ball.

My forced smile burned my lips. I lifted the suitcase in my hand. "Can we come in?"

Seemingly taken aback, my mother blinked out of a trance, then stepped aside. "Of-of course you *may*." I ignored the snide correction. "You've just caught me off guard... I just saw you all at Dylan's birthday dinner. I thought that would be all I'd see of you until Christmas. Thanksgiving, at least."

"Well, here we are."

We shuffled inside, dropping our bags on the floor of the foyer.

"Hey, Grandma," Maisy mumbled, unenthusiastically.

"Hello, dear. What on earth are you all wearing?" Mom asked, once she'd gotten a better look at us.

"We just came from Florida," I told her. "We were on vacation."

"And you couldn't stop to shower? Jesus, Ainsley, you look like farm animals." She glanced at our feet.

I patted Dylan on the shoulder. "Why don't you kids take the bags upstairs and put them in my old room? Then you can take your showers, brush your teeth, and freshen up a bit while I cook us breakfast. Do you remember where it is?"

"Yeah." He lifted his bag. "Dibs on the first shower."

"No fair! I was going to call it," Riley argued, grabbing his own bag and rushing to beat his brother up the stairs.

"Boys!" I chided.

I waited until all three children had disappeared up the stairs and around the corner before addressing my mom. "I'm sorry we've just shown up here. It's a long story, but—"

"You could've at least called," she said stiffly. "What's wrong? Where's Peter?"

"He's not with us. I took the kids to Florida for the week before they went on fall break. We were planning to stay two full weeks, but things changed." I thought it would be best to keep the story straight between what I told my mother and what I'd told the kids. "Peter was supposed to join us, but he got caught up at work." I paused. "You haven't heard from him, have you?"

She eyed me. "Why would I have heard from Peter?" Then her expression grew grim. "You mean you *haven't*?"

"No, I have. He's just really busy with his new project. We drove through a few dead spots overnight, so I wanted to make sure he hadn't called you... Anyway, like I said, I'm sorry we're dropping in on you unannounced. I meant to call, but I...didn't. The kids needed showers and food, and I have a few errands to run. I didn't want to leave them home alone."

She was quiet for a few moments, and I worried she might tell us to leave. Instead, she stepped forward, reaching for my bag. "Better here than your father's."

I closed my eyes with a soft laugh, relieved to be accepted, and nodded. "Thank you."

"I'll fix them breakfast. Lord knows how you always burn things. What do you think they'll want?"

I let the remark roll over me. "Um, what do you have? Cereal, maybe? Oatmeal? I don't want you to go through any trouble. I can throw it together for them."

Before we made our way into the kitchen, she placed my bag at the bottom of the stairs. "Seriously? Oatmeal? Cereal? You know me better than that. You can choose to feed your children like modern vermin in your household, but in my house, our bodies are our temples." In the kitchen, she opened the fridge, tapping a finger to her lips. "We'll do an egg white omelet with spinach for Maisy. And...the same, but I'll add some cheese and turkey bacon for those growing boys." She pulled ingredients from the fridge, and I flinched, my hand going to my wrist involuntarily. I dug a nail into my skin, recalling the numerous times I'd stood in this exact spot and been ridiculed for my food choices and the size of my body.

"No," I said sharply.

She paused, looking at me as if I'd just grown a spare head. "Excuse me?"

"Just...please, Mom. Just please fix them the same thing. Maisy can eat whatever the boys eat." She pursed her lips, preparing for an argument, but I headed it off. "I know how you feel about food, but they're my kids. And they haven't eaten since lunch yesterday, so please. *Please.* Just feed them breakfast and don't talk to Maisy about her food choices."

Her jaw snapped shut, and she placed the food on the countertop with extra force, muttering something that sounded like *ungrateful* under her breath as she turned away from me to dig in a drawer.

"I'm sorry." I stepped forward, placing a hand on the granite island. "I shouldn't have snapped. I'm just tired. We're all tired. It's been a long night. I should be thanking you for letting us visit."

When she turned back to me, there was a weariness in her eyes that matched my own. "You know you're always welcome here, Ainsley. Any of you."

"I know," I told her, though it had only been moments ago that I'd doubted it.

She slammed the drawer shut, spatula in hand, before retrieving a skillet from the cabinet next to the stove. "Is everything okay? Really?"

I sighed, sliding onto the barstool across from her. "Everything's fine, Mom."

She placed the pan on the stove, then moved to the sink to wash her hands. "You know, you never were very good at lying to me."

Oh, I know.

She seemed to read my thoughts, glaring at me over her shoulder. "It's Peter, isn't it? The two of you are having problems?" She shut off the water and turned back to me, drying her hands on a towel she'd pulled from a nearby drawer. She tutted. "Oh, I worried this would happen."

I stared at her in disbelief, then shook my head. "We aren't having issues. Peter and I are...fine."

"*Fine* isn't good." Her brows rose defiantly. "I sensed it at the birthday dinner. Things were...off between the two of you. I said so to your father. Oh, he'll just be devastated to hear this. It's all his fault, isn't it? I told him how bad it was for Peter to see him with his latest floozy. Men always think the grass is greener, don't they?"

"Mom, stop! It's not that. I swear, it isn't. Peter and I are fine. We're *great*. I swear."

She pulled a bowl from a cabinet, opening the carton of eggs without looking at me. "Then why are you here when you have a perfectly good home thirty minutes from here? Why are you here when you've only brought those children into my home when I force you to?" She waved an egg in the air—midcrack—pointing toward the top floor. "You're lying to me, Ainsley, and I want to know why."

I placed my head in my hands, my shoulders drooping. What more could I say? What could I say to my mother or my children? What could I tell them?

For so long, all I'd wanted was a life without secrets and lies, and now, thanks to Peter, I'd found myself being the one doling them out the most. Who had he turned me into?

I inhaled deeply, working to keep my tone even. "You're right."

"Of course I am." She didn't miss a beat.

"Peter and I are...having problems." Sweat beaded at my hairline, my entire body revolting against the truth. I hated myself for admitting it. I hated it for being true.

"An affair?" she asked. "Financial problems?"

"No. Nothing like that. Things have just gotten...stressful."

"As they do."

"And we agreed we needed some time apart."

She cracked another egg, still listening.

"Which was why I took the kids to Florida. But then, he texted me and asked me to come back and talk to him." I lowered my voice. "I don't want the kids to know any of this."

"Of course not," she vowed.

"Dad either," I added.

She paused, apparently deciding how to feel about that, before giving a small smile. "Of course, dear. I can certainly understand why you'd trust me more than your father with an issue like this. I'm happy to watch the kids while you and Peter work on whatever is going on." She turned to the refrigerator, retrieving the spinach and transferring it to a strainer. "He's one of the good ones, you know. You two will work it out."

I nodded, feeling nauseous. "I'm... I'm going to check on the kids, okay?"

"Take your time. Freshen up. Breakfast will be ready when you are."

I slid off of the barstool, making my way across the hardwood floor slowly. I hated being back in this house, but I couldn't focus on that. Now that the kids were safe, I needed to move on to the next step in my plan.

It was time to find my husband.

CHAPTER THREE

AINSLEY

The shower did little to make me feel refreshed. Though my skin and hair were now free of sand and salt, I'd been unable to wash the disgust from my body so easily.

I was repulsed by myself in a way I didn't know was possible.

As someone who'd always lacked the sort of self-love women write memoirs about, this was a new low, even for me. I hated whom Peter had turned me into. Hated how far I'd let myself fall. Not in the way my mother thought I'd let myself go. At that point, I couldn't bring myself to care less about the wrinkles forming near my eyes or the extra weight the stress had added to my hips.

I was disappointed—no, not a strong enough word—I was *furious* with myself for ever letting a man—a monster —control me. For ever letting him make me think my only choice was to do whatever it took to keep him in my life.

For ever letting him believe I was something less than whole without him.

I was a whole person before Peter.

I could be whole again without him.

I *would* be whole again without him.

The sight of the end of our long gravel driveway caused my chest to grow tight. I swallowed, trying to collect saliva in my too-dry throat.

He wasn't going to be there.

He was probably still trying to figure out where we were.

Nevertheless, I reached for the chef's knife I'd stolen from my mother's house, sliding it out of the passenger seat and gripping the handle firmly, eyes peeled for any sight of him.

I eased the car up the driveway slowly, my breath catching in my throat. I had no idea what to expect.

Would the house still be standing?

How much damage had the fire done?

Had he managed to put it out before it took down everything?

Do I hope he did?

The thought appeared as if it were smoke—displaying in my mind for a brief moment and disappearing just as fast.

Did I hope the house was still standing? If I managed to get Peter out of our lives for good, could I ever see moving my children back into it? Could I live there without him, with all the memories we made within those walls?

Would I want to?

The question brought unexpected tears to my eyes, and as I rounded the corner, laying eyes on our home— untouched by any signs of the fire I'd started—an odd mixture of terror and relief spread through my chest.

So, it was still standing.

The garage doors were shut, all the lights inside turned off, and I saw no sign of life anywhere, but that didn't mean he wasn't there. Peter was a rabid dog I'd backed into a corner. For once, I had no way of predicting his next move. I had no idea how far I'd pushed him, how far he'd go to get his revenge.

Slowing the car to a stop, I sat, knife in one hand and phone in the other, waiting to see if he'd appear. The hair on the back of my neck stood at attention, every nerve in my body on high alert. I checked the rearview, then the side mirrors.

When I'd convinced myself he was, in fact, not there and not coming to get me—not yet, anyway—I opened the door to my car and stepped out. I shoved my phone into my pocket and passed the knife to my left hand long enough to wipe my sweaty palm across my jeans.

Then, regripping the weapon, I moved toward the front porch with cautious steps. It was half the size of what it used to be, and I couldn't help thinking of what had caused that.

Better yet, *who* had caused it.

It wasn't so long ago we'd had to work together to solve what I thought would be the biggest problem of our marriage. I thought back then that Stefan would be the end of our issues. That I would force Peter to tell me the truth about everything, that I would tell him I accepted him for who he was and loved him in spite of it all, and that finally we'd break through the wall that had kept us separated.

I had no idea what I was doing back then.

It was nearly a year ago now, but it felt like a lifetime. Two lifetimes, in fact.

Peter was never going to change. Joanna made me realize that. And, when he wouldn't change, I had to. So, I had. And I would continue to. As soon as I'd cleaned up my mess.

Turning back to the task at hand, I slid my house key into the front door, held my breath, and pushed the door open abruptly. I jerked the knife into the air, ready for an attack.

One.

Two.

Three.

Nothing. No one jumped out. No one screamed. No one grabbed me.

I stepped into our house as if I'd just popped out to the grocery store for an hour. The smell hit me instantly —our smell. The scent that had welcomed me home for so long.

I closed the door behind me, moving through the living room with silent footsteps. When I neared the hallway, a new scent hit me.

Smoke.

Or, rather, ash.

Soot.

The bedroom.

I flipped on the hallway light, running a hand along Maisy's door. I couldn't bring myself to open it. Couldn't bring myself to reminisce about the life we'd had in this home just days earlier.

When I reached our bedroom, I held my breath—both because of the strong, smoky scent and my fear of what I'd find—and pushed the door open.

The sight brought tears to my eyes in an instant. The bedroom had taken the brunt of the damage, it was obvious. Everything that had been white—the bedspread, the walls, the ceiling—was now stained black and gray. As if the room had shriveled up and died along with our marriage.

I made my way across the soot-covered floor, still processing the sight of it all. It was unbelievable. Though I'd expected it to be much worse—expected the entire house to be gone, taking my husband with it—looking at even this amount of damage was excruciating.

Had I really expected I'd be okay with destroying my memories? Had I really thought the demolition of my life —the smoldering of everything that had ever mattered to me—would be okay?

That I'd walk away from it unscathed?

The answer was yes.

Yes, at the time I had.

That was what Peter did to me. He made it so nothing in the world mattered. Nothing else but him.

Love him, fight for him, or kill him, he made sure the world only revolved around him.

I turned away and hurried from the room, unable to stand the sight or smell of it any longer, and swiped tears from my eyes angrily.

He wasn't here.

None of this was conducive to my mission.

Peter wasn't here, and standing around crying in the burned-up heap that was once our bedroom wasn't solving anything. I'd made this mess. It was my fault. And now, if I wanted to save my children and myself, I needed to track down my husband and end things once and for all.

If only it were that easy.

CHAPTER FOUR

PETER

It had been a week since my wife tried to kill me, and I still wasn't sure I believed it.

I mean, really, how does one come to grips with the fact that the person they're married to is a monster?

There was no other word for it, try as I might to find one.

Monster.

I couldn't rationalize how the woman I'd shared a home and a bed with for so many years could suddenly seem so different to me. Like a light switch. Like she'd flipped, switching personalities in an instant to become someone I didn't recognize.

Once, I'd seen Ainsley as someone safe—someplace safe. The calm to my storm. But now? Now, she was a storm all her own, and no one was safe.

The next exit showed a sign for a little diner, the kind of hole-in-the-wall place I might once have gone to for an entirely different reason, and I lifted my foot from the accelerator, switching lanes.

I needed to get something in my stomach, coffee if nothing else. A few minutes later, I was pulling into the small diner parking lot. There were a total of five cars in the lot, including mine, and I suspected most were employees.

Walking inside, my suspicions were confirmed. The diner was small, quiet, and smoky. At the far end of the room, a small child sat with a man who must've been her grandfather. She dug into a stack of pancakes hungrily as the man sipped his coffee.

"Just you, honey?" A waitress in a light-blue uniform approached me from around a corner. Her wild and curly graying-blonde hair was pulled up on top of her head in a manner that looked like she'd been playing with an electrical socket, and the red lipstick she wore was too bright and too smeared to appear anything other than sloppy. Though I tried to fight it, I couldn't help thinking of Ainsley then—the red lipstick she wore so perfectly.

I cleared my throat. "Yep. Just me."

"Right this way." She led me toward a booth against the left wall, so I could look out at the parking lot through the oversized window, and placed an enormous laminated menu in front of me. "Know what you want?"

"Erm, coffee, please. And..." I scanned the menu— they had everything from burgers and tacos to pancakes and crepes, but nothing sounded appetizing.

"The sampler's on special today. Just seven ninety-nine." She extended a long, bony finger to point toward the menu. Bacon, hash browns, eggs, sausage, toast, and pancakes.

"Sounds good. I'll take that."

"How do you want your eggs?"

"Scrambled's fine."

"Be right back with your coffee." She took the menu from me, tucking the pencil and notepad in her apron and laid a roll of silverware on the coffee-and-cigarette-stained tabletop.

Once she was gone, I checked in with the little girl and her grandfather again. My breaths slowed as the memories of my children began to take over. It wasn't so long ago that could've been us—them talking nonstop about something I was only half listening to; them asking me to try a bite of their breakfast; their sticky-sweet smiles and fingers; the chocolate-and-whipped-cream mustaches after a particularly sweet treat.

I'd lost track of time—overcome by the memories and overwhelmed by the sadness of knowing they were long gone—when the waitress reappeared and placed a mug of coffee and a bowl full of various creamer options in front of me.

"Thanks." I tore open one of the containers and poured the liquid into my drink, stirring it slowly.

For the past six days, I'd worked tirelessly to track Ainsley down. I'd never been so thankful I'd decided to put in an emergency escape plan, on the off chance something went wrong in that room, though I'd never expected that *something* to be what it was. After escaping the room that day and taking care of a few housekeeping items like burying Joanna's body, I checked the bank account.

After she'd killed our therapist, Ainsley said they were going away, but she hadn't said where. Luckily, the charge to the Panama City hotel was easy enough to track. She thought she was so smart—always one step ahead of me—but this time, I'd proved her wrong. This time, I was the one ahead of her. I'd found them at the hotel, watched how she moved so freely through life, as if she didn't have a care in the world. As if she wasn't a walking, talking husband murderer.

I could've gone after her. Could've chased her down and confronted her right then, but I'd been working on my impulse control. Ironic, isn't it? My impulses were what got us into this mess, and now I wanted to learn to control them?

Hm.

Well, better late than never, I guess.

So, rather than acting, I watched. Observed. Though she tried to hide it, I saw her checking over her shoulder more than once. Was she looking for me then? Or maybe just the police?

Did she worry about that?

I had the feeling my wife never worried much at all.

But she should've.

At least, she should now.

After two days of watching, I sent the text to let her know I'd escaped. I wanted to see how she'd react. Wanted to see the fear in her eyes. Wanted to watch it settle into her bones. I wanted fear and terror and para-

27

noia to permeate every inch of her body, every nerve, every muscle, every cell.

I wanted to be her walking, talking nightmare. To haunt her every waking thought.

And it had worked—possibly better than I'd anticipated.

Within minutes, she'd loaded the kids into the car, stopped at the hotel just long enough to pack their bags into the car, and they'd left. I could've stopped them then, I supposed. And I thought about it. I was hidden in plain sight—my rental car completely unnoticeable when she was watching for our SUV, but I was having entirely too much fun pacing myself.

As long as I knew where she was, there was no need to rush. I could have fun with this.

For once, I'd stay ahead of her.

For once, my wife would be my prey.

CHAPTER FIVE

AINSLEY

The kids knew something was wrong.

I was doing a terrible job fooling them, despite my best effort. When I'd finally made it back to Mom's house, they were sitting together on the couch while Mom flitted about, dusting this and wiping that. Maisy had a book in her lap and Dylan was scrolling through his phone while Riley played a video game on his handheld system.

To someone who didn't know them, they might look normal, but I knew better.

Maisy had been staring at the same page for far too long to actually be reading, Dylan was scrolling so aimlessly I knew he wasn't paying attention, and Riley was losing repeatedly at a game I'd seen him beat a thousand times.

I was hurting them.

I went upstairs, changing into something more comfortable and splashing water over my face before returning to the living room. Practically at once, the kids looked up.

"Hey, Momma." Maisy's smile was soft and hopeful.

I sank down next to her, patting her leg.

"Did you take care of everything?" Dylan asked. "Can we go home now?"

I had no idea what I was going to say or how I was going to explain any of this to them. I only knew I couldn't put this off any longer.

"I—"

"Kids, I think I have some ice cream in the refrigerator. Would you like some?" Mom asked, interrupting me.

"Nah." Maisy moved closer to me.

"I'm okay," Dylan told her.

Riley looked like he might've been prepared to take her up on the offer, but after his siblings' dismissal, he said, "No thanks."

She stared at them, her lips forming a thin line as she waved the white cloth in her hand to fan herself.

"It's okay, Mom." I nodded, understanding what she was doing, though I couldn't quite understand why.

"Could I talk to you for a second, Ainsley?" Her eyes flicked toward the kitchen. "In there."

For a moment, I was twelve years old again, being summoned to another room to be scolded out of earshot of our guests. I blinked back to reality. This wasn't that. I wasn't in trouble. I couldn't be in trouble.

I stood from the couch, patting Maisy's shoulder and offering a reassuring smile. "I'll be right back."

My mother led the way toward the kitchen, and I sat down across from her at the island.

"Ice cream?" I asked, trying to lighten the mood. "Since when do you keep ice cream in the house?"

"I don't." Her lips were stiff. "It was left here by a friend." The way she said *friend* had my curiosity piqued, but I didn't press the issue. Maybe my mother was dating someone new after all. "It's one of those healthy ice creams—no carbs, no sugar, no dairy. I didn't think it should be thrown out." She folded her arms across her chest. "Besides, I was just trying to prevent you from making a terrible mistake."

Cue the dramatics.

"A terrible mistake?"

"You were about to tell the children that Peter has left you, weren't you?"

It was as if she'd spoken a foreign language. It took several seconds for me to comprehend what she'd said. "Um, what? Why would you assume *he* left *me*? Why would you assume *anyone* left *anyone*?"

"That's what you told me, isn't it?"

There was the mother I knew. Right on schedule. She only remembered what she chose to, and it was very rarely accurate.

I scoffed. "No, it isn't what I told you. I said we're taking time apart."

"So, you're separated?"

I hesitated, but there was no use denying it. "We... aren't using those terms exactly, but yes."

My mother fell forward on the counter as if she'd

31

been punched in the stomach. "Oh, god!" She dropped the cloth in her hand, covering her mouth. "Oh, god, Ainsley, what have you done?"

"Why do you assume it's anything I've done?"

She shook her head, resting a cheek against the counter. "Do you have any idea what this will be like for you?"

"What are you talking about?"

"Divorce, Ainsley! Divorce. That nasty little *D* word. I tried to shield you from it as much as possible growing up. I tried to make sure you never saw the worst parts, but still, I couldn't protect you from everything. You see what the divorce did to me. Here I am, struggling to keep up with the house and all the bills your father left behind. Do you see your father struggling? Well, you won't. Because divorced men have it easy. They aren't tainted goods like we are. You mark my words, if you give Peter the chance to find out he has options that don't involve coming home every night to a nagging wife and chores, he'll surely take it. Whatever you have to do, whatever you have to say, you make this right." She wagged her finger at me. "You make this right today. Before Peter has a chance to realize what an opportunity he has in front of him. Because he will. And then..." She sighed, shaking her head with a haunted look in her eyes. "Then it'll be too late."

Bitterness filled my chest. "You have no idea what you're talking about."

"Don't I?" she challenged, squaring her shoulders to mine. "Take a good long look at my life, honey. Unless you want this to be yours, I suggest you start watering the grass at home and making sure your husband is taken care of."

I stood, indignation filling me. She had no idea what I'd done in order to make my marriage work. She had no idea what I'd sacrificed all in the name of making my husband happy.

I was my mother's daughter, after all.

But I had someone new to think about now. A daughter of my own. And I would be mortified to learn she'd done even half of what I had in order to save a marriage with a man who didn't deserve her.

And Peter didn't deserve me.

"I know you fought to keep Dad around after he found out about your affair—"

She fell forward again with a dramatic gasp. "You just had to dig the knife in on that, didn't you?"

"I know you tried, Mom," I went on. "I do. And I know Dad has gone on to build what you probably think is a pretty nice life. But not every divorce is that way. And not every marriage is worth saving—"

"But *yours* is—"

"You know nothing about my marriage," I spat, my tone more biting than I'd meant it to be.

She pulled back from the counter in shock.

I put my hands up in surrender. "I'm sorry, but you don't. Believe me, I have tried. I have tried everything I know to do. But I will not put myself second for the sake of my marriage. I will not put those kids second. Maybe that's the life you want for me, but it's not what I want for my children. It's not what I would want for Maisy. And if our marriage isn't what I'd want for her, then what am I even doing?"

"Kids don't know any better. They don't see the unhappiness. No one's truly happy." She waved it off as if happiness were as realistic as sprouting wings and flying away. "What those kids need is two parents who will stay together no matter what. They need stability. Have I taught you nothing?"

"*I* can give them stability. Trust me, I am much more stable without Peter than I ever was with him."

"I doubt that." She shook her head, turning away from me. "Maisy needs her father. Those boys need a good male role model. If you let Peter leave, it's pure self-ishness. If you can live with that, fine, but don't trick yourself into believing you're doing it for the kids, Ainsley. You're doing it for yourself. Because it's the easiest thing for you. If you can live with that, I guess there's nothing left to say." With that, she picked up the cloth once again and stormed from the room, leaving me to process everything she'd said.

It had been a mistake to come here, that much was obvious. But what choice did I have? Where could we go?

CHAPTER SIX

PETER

My wife never failed to surprise me.

She'd been by the house—evidenced by the bedroom door left open and the black footprints she'd tracked down the hall. It was okay. I'd have to have the carpets cleaned anyway, along with repairing the damage her little tantrum had done to our bedroom. But, these things could be fixed. Forgiven.

We were all entitled to a bit of less-than-perfect behavior now and again.

I pulled what was left of the duvet and sheets from the bed, shoving them into the trash bag in my hand.

The mattress was in rough shape. It would have to be discarded.

What a shame, really.

So many good times on that thing.

I sighed. She'd started the fire in the bedroom, and I had to believe that was on purpose. She'd wanted me to know she was torching our marriage—our family—right along with our home.

But, this time, I'd saved it.

Saved our home, if not our bed.

And, given enough time, I'd save our family too.

With the sheets tied safely in the bag, I tossed it aside and began shoving the mattress from the bed frame. The box spring beneath the mattress had minimal damage and the flooring underneath was untouched. Gray smoke had stained nearly every other surface in the room.

I pulled out the vacuum and set to work.

Whenever I brought them all home, I wanted to be sure there was no sign of what had happened here. It would be like nothing ever happened at all. There was no need for the reminder, and I doubted the kids knew anything about it in the first place.

She'd been careful about her timing, waiting to light the bed on fire until she was walking out the door, from the looks of it. I'd bet anything the kids were already in the car and she'd claimed she had to come inside to get something.

I still didn't know how she'd managed to throw the burning cloth into the room with me without the kids noticing, but it was the smell of smoke that had woken me up—my body suddenly on high alert.

She hadn't counted on that.

The sheer human will to live.

I would've known to account for it. I'd seen it with my own victims—the way they fought back with everything they had, even when I'd been sure they were inches from death.

Ainsley didn't have the experience I did.

She didn't understand there was nothing a person wouldn't do to keep on living. She didn't yet know I would've done anything to get our lives back to the way they were.

She wanted it, too.

Maybe it didn't seem that way, when looking from the outside, but I knew my wife better than that. I could see what she wasn't saying.

Sure, she'd drugged me hours before and counted on the fact that I'd sleep through it all. But was she really counting on that? She'd torn Jim to shreds, stared into his eyes as he bled to death in front of her, but she couldn't stand to face me as she ended my life.

That counted for something in my book.

She just needed some time to rest, to recenter, and come to terms with all that had happened. We'd both made mistakes—with Joanna, with each other—but when it counted, we were good together. With the coach, with Stefan, with Jim. Ainsley and I were a team—the best team—and when she'd had a chance to clear her head, she'd see that.

I'd keep an eye on her until then and, when she was ready, I'd bring her home.

With or without the use of rope.

CHAPTER SEVEN

AINSLEY

The kids slept with me that night.

No. *Sleep* is a generous term.

The kids and I tossed and turned in the bedroom I'd grown up in. Maisy and Riley shared the full-size bed, while Dylan and I slept on separate air mattresses. There was a spare bedroom just down the hall, but I couldn't bring myself to leave them. Lucky for me, they seemed to feel the same way.

The next morning, I was stiff and sore from sleeping on the slowly deflating mattress. I stood under the warm water of the shower for an extra few minutes, allowing it to ease the ache in my bones.

An hour later, I'd dressed in one of the nicest outfits in my suitcase and put on a light layer of makeup before straightening my hair. Despite my life falling apart, I couldn't let anyone sense my weakness. There are few things that appear stronger than a woman who seems put together.

They were still sleeping when I walked in from the bathroom and planted a quick kiss on each of their foreheads. When one of Dylan's eyes fluttered open, I whispered, "Go back to sleep. I'm going to run into town for a bit. Watch out for your brother and sister for me, okay? Call me if you need anything."

He nodded with a seriousness that made my stomach seize. Though he didn't understand what was happening, though I'd managed to avoid telling them anything concrete, he was unofficially taking on the role of man of the house. I could see it there in his golden eyes.

"We'll be fine."

"I know. I'll be back soon," I promised, walking out the door without another word.

As I passed the living room where Mom was sitting and drinking her morning tea, I lifted my hand with a passing wave toward her and kept moving. She lowered her mug. "Where are you off to so early?"

"Work." I refused to stop long enough to talk. "I'll be back in a few hours. The kids are still sleeping."

"Don't they have school?"

"No. I told you, they're on fall break."

I pulled open the door and stepped outside, releasing a heavy breath as I made my way toward the car. For the entire car ride—twenty minutes longer than it would've taken me from home—I rode in silence, making a list of everything I needed to do that day.

Work was at the top of my to-do list, though not because I was planning to return just yet. I still had a week of my vacation left, and I needed to make the most of it.

I walked into the branch just after they opened; the familiarity and utter coolness of the place were in perfect juxtaposition, just like the house had been. It's like that sometimes. When the place you're visiting hasn't changed a bit, but you have. When you're so different from who you were the last time you were there—be it a day or ten years ago—that nothing feels right or normal or familiar anymore.

"Well, hey. I didn't think you'd be here until next week," Tara said, hand on the pronounced bump under her blouse.

"Oh, I'm not here," I told her. "Not officially. I'm just running a few errands."

Brendan walked out of the vault with a cupcake in his hands. Upon seeing me, he froze, and I watched him contemplate hiding the dessert.

"Hey..." he said softly, keeping his distance.

"It's okay. I've already seen it." I didn't have time to remind them I didn't like for them to eat behind the counter in front of customers. "I need to make a large withdrawal."

Tara passed me a slip as Brendan moved closer.

Finally at his station, he hid the cupcake and turned his attention to me, a too-bright smile on his lips. "How was your trip? Looks like you got some sun."

"Yeah, a little bit." I scribbled down my signature on the slip and passed it back. "I want to leave twenty-five dollars in each account. Transfer everything else into this account and then withdraw it all except for the twenty-five in there, too. I'm not sure how much that is exactly."

Tara stared at the slip, then began signing into her system. Once she'd pulled up our account, she stared at me strangely, then turned to Brendan. "How much do you have in your drawer?"

"Not much. Mrs. O'Leary cleared me out. How much do you need?" He leaned over to check the screen. "Yeah, I don't have that much. I can give you a thousand, maybe."

"I just took in the deposit from Leo's, but it's mostly twenties." She looked back at me. "Do you want this in hundreds or..."

"Yeah, as big of bills as you can do it, please. I don't mind a few twenties, though." It wasn't as if we were talking about massive amounts of money. Even with our savings accounts, it would be less than five thousand.

"We'll have to get into the vault for it," she said, wincing.

"That's fine. I can wait."

She nodded toward Brendan, who grabbed his keys and jogged to the back.

"How are you feeling?" I hated making small talk when I had so much else going on, but it felt rude not to at least ask.

She seemed to relax at the question, rubbing her belly again. "Growing by the hour, it feels like." She laughed, then raised a brow. "You aren't leaving us, are you?"

"Hm?" The question caught me off guard.

"Taking all your money out and hitting the road." She chuckled awkwardly.

"Oh." I sighed. "No, not at all. Just a big expense. Hey, Peter hasn't been in, has he?"

She looked worried then. "I don't think so."

"Just making sure. He said he'd let me know if he made it by before I had the chance, but I hadn't heard from him. I guess if the money hasn't already been withdrawn, that answers my question." I waved off the question. "Anyway, I have a few things to take care of in my office. Will you let me know when you have the money ready?"

"Sure." Her smile was small and decidedly *un*sure, but she gave it and I walked away.

In my office, I pulled up and checked my email, scanning through things I could ignore until I returned and responded to the few urgent matters. Next, I picked up the phone and dialed my boss's office number.

"This is Tina."

"Tina, hey, it's Ainsley Greenburg."

"Ainsley, hey." She paused. "Are you already back from vacation? I thought I still had Mackenzie covering your branch..."

"I'm still out for the next week. Actually, that's why I'm calling. I wanted to see about taking a few extra days off." She was quiet for a moment, the silence dragging out, so I added, "I have the time. And I'll work out whatever schedule the branch needs with the staff. I'm sure Kenzie or Becca wouldn't mind covering."

"What's going on? Is everything okay?"

I nodded, though she couldn't see me. "Yeah, it's just a family thing. With my kids."

"Well, how long are you asking for?"

"Maybe an extra week, I'm not really sure. I'd like to put in for all of the week after next, and then we can check in that Friday to see where I'm at." Guilt weighed on me. "I know this isn't convenient. Trust me, I do. But you know me. You know I wouldn't ask if it wasn't important. My family needs me right now. I haven't ever asked for time off like this, not even when I had the kids. I come to work no matter what I'm dealing with at home. But this is important."

She sighed heavily, and I could hear her typing something. "Yeah, okay. I know. It's fine. We'll manage. I'll call Mackenzie to see if she can still cover for you for a few more days, and then maybe some of the other managers can cover a day or two. But keep me in the loop, okay? I'm counting on you to be back the week after that unless I hear from you."

"Of course."

"And make sure to put in the request officially, so I can approve it."

"I'm doing that right now."

"Thanks, Ainsley," she said, though she didn't sound thankful at all.

"Thank you so much."

"Hey—" She stopped me just before I was able to hang up.

"Yeah?"

"I just wanted to say I hope everything's okay with

the family." Her tone was softer then, almost apologetic. "Keep us posted, okay? Let me know if there's anything I can do."

So, I wasn't too deep in hot water after all. "I will. Thanks, Tina."

A knock on my door startled me as I ended the call and, when I looked up, Tara was standing in the doorway with an envelope in her hand. "Here you go." She passed it to me.

"Oh, you didn't have to bring this out here. I would've come and gotten it."

"I know. We've been slow, and I've been wanting to talk to you anyway."

I froze, my breathing hitching. "Yeah?" I knew what she was going to say before she'd said it. Before she'd ever spoken a word. I recognized that nervous look in her eye; it was one I'd seen before, and it never brought good news.

She sank into the chair in front of my desk as I tucked the money away. "I, um, I hate to do this right now, because I know you're not officially here, but...I need to put in my notice."

"You're quitting?"

She gave a guilty chuckle, rubbing her stomach again as if to remind me of it. "I'm sorry. It's just...we've always planned for me to stay home once we have kids. I thought I'd still work through my pregnancy, but at my last appointment, my blood pressure was a little high. They're talking about putting me on bed rest if I can't get it down and, well, Joel is really worried about my stress levels. It took us so long to actually get pregnant. I just don't want to mess this up." She had tears in her eyes as she said the last sentence, making the guilt I was already feeling swell to double its size.

"Of course." I put a hand out across the desk, patting the wood thoughtfully. "I understand." Though it was the worst possible timing in the world, I did understand. I cared about Tara. I'd known her for years, and at one time, I'd considered her a close friend.

"I'm going to miss this place." She glanced around the room sadly, sniffling.

"Well, would you rather use FMLA leave for a few weeks to see how you feel? I can help you put in that request."

"No. If I use up that time, I wouldn't have it around for after the baby's born. It's only twelve weeks, and I still have a long time to go. Plus, if something were to happen and I had to get put in the hospital, I'd run out of time and lose my job anyway. It's not worth the risk. I'd rather just put in my notice now, so I don't have to stress about coming back before I'm ready."

"I understand." I paused, tapping my finger against the desktop. "I'm really happy for you."

A deep smile spread across her lips. "Thank you."

"Okay, well, are you putting in a full two weeks?"

"Yeah. Two weeks from today is fine. I've already been training Brendan on my reports and LeAnn has been helping with shipments, so the two of them can train whoever comes in next."

I nodded, a wave of heat washing over me like air

from a dryer. Life never stopped, did it? Not even when your world was ending. "Okay. Perfect. Thanks, Tara. Just...um..." I couldn't think straight. "Just be sure to send me an email and CC Jenn from HR on it, so we officially have it in writing." I paused. "You're on Joel's insurance, aren't you?"

"I will be, once I leave. His company will only let him add me if I'm uninsured."

"Good." I tried to slow my breathing as my head throbbed. "Great. Okay, then."

"Okay." She stood, patting her legs. "I'll, uh, I'll see you next week, right? We can talk more."

"Mhm." I couldn't say any more, couldn't correct her. The stress coursing through me was making it difficult to catch my breath. Training a new teller was going to be hard enough, but training someone to do all of the head teller responsibilities would take weeks, if not months. I had no time at all if I was going to miss all of the next two weeks, but what choice did I have?

At one point, I'd summoned the strength to work through a literal murder investigation, but I couldn't do that this time. My children needed me too badly.

I closed out my email and stood from my desk, picking up my purse and double-checking that the envelope of cash was still there.

I needed to take care of my children.

For now, the rest would have to wait.

CHAPTER EIGHT

PETER

I checked off a list of possibilities for where my wife might be. She was home now, that much was obvious, so the list of places I'd need to check was growing smaller.

I drove to Glennon and Seth's first, though I didn't truly believe she'd be naive enough to go there. But maybe... No doubt she still thought I was seeking her out in Florida, or on my way back up the same path she'd traveled.

Seth and Glennon's was as empty as it had been for months. Ainsley's car wasn't in the bank parking lot, and the school secretary said the kids weren't there.

The list was dwindling.

She had nowhere to go. Nowhere to run to.

No family she could count on.

Thanks to me, her only friends were now halfway across the country.

I was it.

She needed me.

And soon enough, I'd get her to admit that.

I'd checked the bank account that morning—the credit cards, too—but there were no new transactions. No hotel or restaurant charges. Wherever she was, she was lying low. I had to respect that.

But soon enough, I'd find her.

I was a bloodhound on her scent, and I'd run myself ragged until she was home with me. And she would be home with me. Once she'd calmed down. Once her fit had been thrown and her anger had subsided.

She needed me, maybe more than I needed her. I'd learned that recently, and now I was realizing she could use some reminding.

Luckily, I was up for the task, and there was just one place left on my list to check.

CHAPTER NINE

AINSLEY

With the cash I'd withdrawn in hand, I stopped by the store. I'd gone a little overboard, but the clothes we had in our bags were meant for Florida weather and I planned to take us somewhere much cooler next. I'd picked up a box of hair dye, too—a painful purchase both because I'd always loved my red hair and because I hated how damaging box dye was, but I didn't have a choice. Back at Mom's, I'd dye it dark and cut it to just below my chin. The fact that Peter had always loved my long hair was a sweet little bonus.

With new hair, I'd feel safer about moving through our town without being noticed. He'd never expect me to be so drastic. It would buy me time and security. At least until I managed to find him and decide my next move.

My phone buzzed in my pocket as I slammed the trunk of the car shut. I pulled it free as I pushed the cart into the corral. Seeing Mom's name on my screen caused my throat to tighten. I swiped my thumb across the screen and pressed it to my ear.

"Mom? Is everything okay?"

"Yes, yes, everything's fine." My thoughts jumbled, the tension disappearing from my neck in an instant.

"Oh, thank God, I—"

"Peter stopped by."

I gulped down a breath, sure I'd misheard. "*Who* did?"

"Peter. He wanted to see the kids."

Snapping back to reality, I rushed around the side of the car and grabbed the door handle, jumping inside. "Did you let him? Is he still there?"

"He's outside. I wasn't sure what you wanted me to—"

"Listen to me." I buckled myself in with one hand, searching desperately for my keys in my purse with the other. My fingers connected with the cool metal, and I jerked them out. "Mom, do not let Peter inside the house, okay? Whatever you do..." I shoved the keys into the ignition, missing the hole once, twice, and a third time before they clicked into place. I turned them, starting the car and lurching forward.

"Well, I didn't let him in, but I really think—"

"No. *No.* I'm not asking what you think. I'm telling you not to let him inside. Did you talk to him? Did you tell him we're staying there?"

"I haven't told him anything. For goodness' sake, stop acting as if this is life or dea—"

"Just keep the kids inside. Do *not* let him in. Do not

tell him we're staying there. Tell him you haven't heard from me and that he should call me. Whatever you do—"

"Yes, yes, I get it. Don't let him inside. You always were one for dramatics, weren't you?"

I let the comment roll over me. "I'll be there in forty minutes." I mashed the accelerator, hoping to arrive sooner than that. I needed to count on my mother to protect the most important things in the world to me, but the sad truth was, I didn't know if I could do it.

"I have to go, Ainsley."

"What? What are you talking about? Why?"

She released a sigh as if the weight of the world were on her shoulders. "Because Peter is at the door again."

"Wait, Mom—"

But it was no use. The call had ended, and the car was filled with a painful silence. I could only assume the worst about the situation as I sped around a curve.

I pressed the button on my steering wheel that activated voice prompts.

"Please say a command."

"Call Peter," I shouted.

"Calling Peter."

The line rang, and I held my breath.

It was the first time either of us had tried to call the other since everything had happened. I was crossing the one line we hadn't yet crossed, breaking the sort of unspoken pact I never wanted to break first.

Once we spoke, things were going to get messy. I just needed to keep my head clear. But this couldn't wait.

The phone went to voicemail after just three rings.

Which meant he wasn't actually looking for me.
He was after the kids.

CHAPTER TEN

PETER

Seeing Ainsley's name on my screen was enough to send me over the edge. I worried about what I'd do —both for my kids and myself. If she was calling, it meant she was finally ready to talk, but maybe I wasn't.

Maybe she should've tried to talk a week ago rather than shoving a needle in my neck.

I'd thought I was ready for this, but I wasn't. I needed time. I needed to breathe. Because the last thing I wanted to do was lose control on my wife, and I was eerily close to that already.

Back at the house, I zipped around the bedroom. It was cleaner than before, with everything I could get rid of out of the way, the carpets vacuumed and shampooed, but still, the evidence of what she'd done lingered. The scent of the damage, of the smoke, was still present throughout the house. In the mirror, I could still see the faint bruising she'd left on my neck from injecting me over and over again.

She'd left quite a mess, and I'd been the dutiful husband, cleaning it up without complaint. But now... now she thought she had the right to call me out of the blue and expect an answer?

Maybe that's what made me the angriest...

The audacity of it all. I'd driven around all this time searching for her, and now that I'd finally tracked them down, now she wanted to call me? I didn't think so.

I tossed my suitcase on the floor and began stuffing it with clothing just as my phone buzzed again. This time, when I pulled it from my pocket and checked the screen, it was the office number that was displayed.

Fuck.

"Hello?"

"Hi, Mr. Greenburg, it's Melodie." My assistant's voice was birdlike and too high pitched, even more so over the phone, but she was incredibly unattractive—with features that didn't fit her face and a boyish haircut that meant I could do my job around her without ever getting distracted.

"Hi, Melodie. Everything okay?"

"Well, um, Miss Miller wanted me to call and see if you'd had a chance to check your email since yesterday. They're waiting on your approval before they can move forward on the Haverman project. I told her you were off this week, but—"

"No, it's fine. I haven't had a chance to look yet, but I'll do that right now, okay? Tell Gina—er, tell Miss Miller—that I'll have it signed off by the end of the day."

"Okay, sir. Thank you, sir."

"Thanks, Melodie."

I ended the call and pulled up the email on my phone, trying to read the blueprint on the too-small screen. I pinched and zoomed, moving it around to double-check the measurements. It wasn't the kind of care I promised to all our clients, but I was sort of in the middle of something and I trusted Gina and Beckman. It was more of a formality than anything to get my approval.

I responded to the email quickly.

Looks great. If you need anything else, call me. I'm not checking emails this week. Thanks.

With that, I pressed send and returned to packing.

Leave it to work to get in the way of a crisis. The world doesn't ever stop needing things from you, does it?

For now, at least, it would have to wait. I was going back to my mother-in-law's. I'd wait all night or longer if that's what it took. I would catch Ainsley—I'd be the one to do it, on my terms, not hers—and I'd bring her home. If it was the last thing I did.

CHAPTER ELEVEN

AINSLEY

I pulled into the driveway and brought the car to a stop with a racing heart and sweaty palms. There was a truck I didn't recognize parked in front of the house, though it didn't belong to us. Who else could be there, though? A lump formed in my throat as I stepped out of the car and moved up the walk, already preparing myself for the worst.

Bloody images filled my mind, tormenting me. Had he hurt them? What would I find walking into that house? I squared my jaw.

He wouldn't hurt them.

My husband was a lot of things, but I didn't believe he was the type of monster who'd hurt our children. He loved them. No matter how unhinged he was, no matter how much he wanted to hurt me, I couldn't believe he would take it out on them.

So, if anything, I hoped he'd just take them.

It would be the one thing in the world he could do to hurt me beyond repair.

Take away my children, Peter, hurt me that way, but please don't hurt them.

I forced the thought away as I twisted the handle and stepped inside. I checked behind the door, then around the room before shutting it firmly and moving forward.

I inhaled deeply, trying to detect a hint of blood or his cologne, but there was nothing. No signs he'd been there at all.

Maybe the car belonged to a neighbor.

Maybe one of my mother's friends, though I couldn't imagine her having friends of any kind. Halfway through the living room, I heard a sound that sent a bolt of lightning through my veins.

Maisy's laughter.

Whom was she laughing at? I knew one person who could make her laugh above all else. I darted toward the sound, rounding the corner into the living room, and froze.

Mom's smile disappeared when she saw me. "Oh, hello, honey. Have you met Matt?"

Matt, apparently, was the man standing in the middle of my mother's kitchen talking to my daughter across the counter. He appeared to be several years younger than me—early twenties, I'd guess—with thick brown, wavy hair, kind eyes, and a barely there five o'clock shadow. He smiled at me, his eyes lingering on mine for longer than necessary, and an embarrassing warmth spread through my stomach. Then he looked back at Maisy, who was practically giddy, watching him the way I'd seen her watch the boys in her favorite bands.

"Um, no..." I moved forward, touching my daughter's arm. *What in the child bride is this?* "What's going on?" Where was Peter?

"Sorry." Matt held out his hand, making too-intense eye contact with me again. Heat rushed to my cheeks. "I'm your new neighbor. I just moved in across the street and came by to introduce myself."

I extended my hand stiffly. Our skin had barely touched when the flutters spread through my extremities. What the hell was happening to me? I pulled my arm back abruptly, with too much force, and tucked a piece of hair behind my ear to mask the movement. "Not *my* neighbor. I don't live here. *We* don't live here." I gestured toward Maisy.

"Oh, I'm sorry. I thought—"

"Well, they're living here right now, anyway," my mother said, batting her eyelashes at him and swatting his arm. He still hadn't taken his eyes off of me. I looked away. "I was just telling Matt that you work at a bank downtown. He worked in banking, too. Can you believe that?"

"Small world," I said halfheartedly, running my hands through Maisy's hair to keep myself busy.

"He's from California," Maisy told me, her eyes as wide as if she'd said he was from the moon. "He used to live at the beach."

"*Near* the beach," he corrected, then took a step closer to me. His voice lowered, as if he were only speaking to me. "And I used to work in banking, but not anymore. It was great, though." He paused, waiting for me to respond, but I had nothing to say. I took a step back, keeping myself between him and Maisy. Finally seeming to notice my discomfort, he backed off, turning his attention back to my daughter. "Anyway, I was just telling Maisy about the time I walked right past Tom Hanks and had no idea until I got home and realized why he looked so familiar. I just waved at him like he was some random guy."

Maisy laughed again. "Can you imagine?" She sighed, biting into a frozen peach from the bowl in front of her. "No one famous ever comes around here."

"We live outside of Nashville, and we're here all the time." I gestured around us, though it wasn't really true. I was in Nashville daily for work, Peter too, but the kids only came if it was for something specific or if we were visiting my parents. "Plenty of famous people live near us," I told her.

"Yeah, but we never see them. And, even if you do, Nashville has this unspoken rule that you can't approach them. My friend saw Taylor Swift at the mall once and no one even believes her."

"They're just normal people, Maise." I stepped closer, resting my hands on the counter. "Same as you and me."

"You should listen to your mom. That's a way cooler

way of looking at it than I did," Matt agreed, pointing at me, though I didn't need him to back me up with my own daughter. I shot a steely glance his way, and he lowered his hand and averted his eyes, his own cheeks flushing pink. He scratched the back of his neck. "Anyway, I'm sorry to have interrupted. I just wanted to come by and introduce myself and say if you need anything, let me know."

"Well, you weren't interrupting at all. Are you sure you won't have some sangria before you go? I just made a fresh pitcher." My mom was practically unrecognizable, smiling and fawning all over this stranger.

"Oh, no, thank you though. It sounds delicious, but I've got to get back to unpacking. I just happened to see you outside and thought now was as good a time as any. And I wanted to warn you about Sampson, too. If he ever gets annoying, just let me know. This is the first time he's had a yard, so I'm sure he'll be excited for a few days, but I'll do my best to keep him quiet."

"Oh, he's no bother at all. I just love dogs."

This was the same mother who'd once told me we could never have animals because they brought "fleas, worms, and filth" wherever they went.

"Sampson's a Great Dane." Maisy filled me in.

I nodded, unsure of what to say and ready for this stranger to get out of this house.

He stepped back, moving away from the counter with a final nod. "Alright, well, it was great to meet you, Adele." He shook Maisy's hand. "Maisy." Then he locked eyes with me again, suddenly too close. "So nice to meet you, Ainsley. I'm...I'm sure I'll be seeing you around."

I nodded, uncharacteristically at a loss for words.

Luckily for me, Mom was having no such shortage. "So nice to meet you, Matt. I didn't ask, but is that short for Matthew?" She was at his side in an instant, eager to stop his attempts at escape.

"Nah, it's short for Leonard."

Mom hesitated and Matt guffawed, much to Maisy's delight. "Sorry, yeah, it's for Matthew."

"Leonard would be cool," Maisy said.

"Maisy's cooler." He patted her head.

"Mom, you want to walk Matt out?" I asked abruptly, interrupting their laughter.

"That's not necessary." Matt tucked his hands in his pockets. "Sorry, again, for...interrupting." He held my gaze for a half second more, something warm in his eyes that made me feel dizzy, then turned toward the living room.

"Don't be silly. Of course I'll walk you out." Mom rounded the island and crossed the room.

He chuckled, waiting for her to catch up with him. "They warned me about this Southern hospitality, Ms. Adele."

"Oh, just Adele, please." She took hold of his arm, leading the way toward the door. To my dismay, he looked back at me over his shoulder just once more, catching me watching him, and offered a small smile and a wave.

I turned my attention to Maisy, and once they'd left the room, I ran a hand through her hair again, unsure of what to say.

"Are you okay? You look like you're going to be sick," she said, taking another bite of her peach.

I touched my cheeks, the warmth of them burning my palms. "I could ask you the same thing. Is everything okay here?"

She nodded slowly, brows drawn down. "Um, yeah. Why?" She swirled her spoon around the bowl in front of her.

Had my mother told her Peter was there? It didn't seem like it, and I didn't want to bring it up if she hadn't in case she expected to see him.

"That was just kind of weird," I said eventually, as I heard the front door shut.

"What was?"

"The neighbor." I tilted my head in the direction he'd gone. "You didn't think so?"

"I don't know. I thought he was really cool, actually."

"And much too old for you."

"Ew, Mom!" She stuck out her tongue with disgust. "He's like...an adult. What are you talking about? You thought I *liked* him, liked him?"

I shrugged, forcing the worry out of my chest as if clawing it with my bare hands. Maisy was a child. Not every man was out to get her. Was my perception tarnished by everything that had happened with her coach?

"I'm only teasing," I said, waving away her worry,

then crossed the room to retrieve a glass from the cabinet. I filled it with water as we waited for my mother to return. "What have you been up to all day?"

"Reading," she said, her mouth full of fruit. "Grandma said she wants to take me on a walk around the neighborhood later."

"What?" I wasn't sure I'd heard her over the sound of the ice hitting my glass.

She repeated herself. "A walk. For exercise or whatever. Maybe you could go with us."

"No. You're not going to walk around the neighborhood with your grandmother. We're leaving today."

Her eyes brightened. "We are?"

"Mhm. Now, finish eating and run upstairs and tell your brothers to get their bags ready."

She shoved the last few bites of her fruit into her mouth and placed the bowl in the sink, obviously in just as much of a hurry as I was to get out of there.

As she jogged out of the room, she nearly ran into my mother, who jumped back with a start and gasped. "Whoa, where are you off to in such a hurry?"

"Sorry, Grandma," Maisy said, not bothering to explain where she was going as she jogged up the stairs.

"What was that—"

"Where is Peter?" I cut her off, placing my glass of water down.

"What? Oh, oh, right. He left."

"He left?" I folded my arms across my chest. "When?"

"Well, I didn't let him inside, and he left. I didn't check the time, for goodness' sake."

"And you didn't think to call and tell me that?" I huffed, my eyes traveling the room as disbelief swam through me. "Do you have any idea how worried I've been? I could've gotten into an accident. I could've gotten a speeding ticket—"

"Well, I didn't ask you to speed over here." Her indignant stare pierced me.

"I thought my children were in danger." My heart pounded in my ears.

"Why on earth would you think that? I was with them. It was their father at the door, not the bogeyman." She paused, studying me. "Is... Is Peter trying to hurt you? Has he done something to hurt the children?" She covered her agape mouth with long, spindly fingers.

"I—um, well, no. Not exactly. It's...it's complicated. I'm worried..." I lowered my voice, moving toward her in an effort to keep the kids from overhearing this part in particular. "I'm worried he'll try to take the kids from me if he can get to them."

"Why would he do that?" She didn't look convinced.

"To hurt me," I admitted. It was the first honest thing I'd said to my mother in so long. "He really wants to hurt me, Mom. And the kids are the best way to do that."

She was quiet for a long while, her eyes dancing between mine. She opened her mouth, as if prepared to say something, then closed it again. Finally, she said, "Sweetheart, Peter loves you. He's always loved—"

"*No.*" I shut her down. I'd bared my soul to her, told

her something I'd never told anyone else. I needed her to understand. To believe me. To trust me. But she wouldn't. Of course, she wouldn't. This was the same mother who'd berated me my entire life, made me question my own judgments and opinions, and even taken away my right to form opinions or make decisions for as long as she could. Why would I think she'd be any different now? "No. Just stop, Mom, okay? I appreciate you letting us stay here, but this was a mistake. We're going to go—"

"Oh, Ainsley, don't be like that—"

"It's fine." I started toward the stairs, but she stepped in front of me. Just then, a knock sounded at the door. Panic gripped my organs.

"Ms. Adele?"

I heard his voice through the door—unsure whether to be relieved or even more worried. Why was he back so soon? What did he want?

Mom eyed me, then moved away, crossing the room and opening the door. "Matt? Did you decide on some sangria after all?"

He was out of breath, his forehead gleaming with sweat. "Sorry, no. I don't mean to bother you again." He wasn't looking at her. Instead, he was watching me over her shoulder. "Ainsley, is this your car out in the driveway?"

"Yes. Why?" I moved toward the door.

He winced, wiping his brow with the back of his hand. "You've got a flat tire."

"What?" My heart thudded in my chest. "How?"

"I was getting ready to leave when I noticed it. It looks like you hit a nail." He stepped back, clearing a path for me to see for myself. I peered out the door and into the driveway. Sure enough, my front tire was flat and resting on the rim. "I can fix it if you want. Do you have a spare?"

"In the trunk. I..." I tried to think back. Had I hit something on the way over? I was in such a rush it was entirely possible.

"Do you have the keys to pop your trunk? I'm happy to change it for you."

"That's okay. I can call a mechanic."

He waved me off. "A mechanic will charge you way too much. I can have it fixed in just a few minutes. It's no trouble."

I hesitated.

"For goodness' sake, Ainsley, just give him the keys. I don't know where her manners are. It's very kind of you to offer, Matt." Mom beamed from beside me.

"It's very kind," I agreed. "But I'm sure you have better things to do with your day."

"It's not a problem, honestly. It'll just take a few minutes. Do you have a tire iron and jack?"

"I'm...not sure. I think so." I heard the kids moving overhead, reminding me that we should be leaving any minute. Peter could come back. What if he did and we were stuck here with no car? I grabbed the keys from the table next to the door. "Thank you. Really. I appreciate it."

"Sure thing. I'm happy to help." He smiled at me, his

eyes lighting up, and held out his hand. When I passed the keys to him, his touch lingered on my skin for a moment too long. My breathing hitched, the stress of the moment melting away for only a second.

I pulled back. "Thank you, " I repeated, tucking my hand in my pocket as if concealing evidence.

"Sure thing. I'll, uh... I'll get to work, then."

I nodded. "I'll be right out."

With that, he turned away, and I watched him approaching the car and popping the trunk. I walked toward the stairs. "Maise, will you bring my stuff down when you come?" I didn't want to leave Matt with our car unattended for long, but there was no time to waste. Every second we stayed there was a second he might return.

"Coming!" she called down.

"So, you're still leaving?" Mom asked, her arms folded across her chest.

"We don't have a choice, Mom." I moved back to the window, watching Matt as he worked to get the tire from its rim.

"Of course you do. I kept him away, didn't I? I did what you asked. You may not agree with my decisions or the way I do things, but you're safe here. The kids are safe here. I just think you're making a huge mistake—"

I spun around, cutting her off. "I have made several mistakes, Mother. But this is the first time in my life that I'm not making any. I'm trying to fix the mistakes I did make. Please, just...just let us get our things, let Matt finish with the tire, and then we'll be out of your hair."

I slipped past her again as the children came into view and, this time, she let me go.

There was nothing left to be said. Nothing left to be done.

I needed to get my children and run before my husband came back. It was only a matter of time.

CHAPTER TWELVE

PETER

With my bag packed, I loaded up the rental car and headed out. Driving down the long, wooded driveway always made me think of the early days of picking out our land.

I'd been hell-bent on getting acreage for...*obvious*... reasons, but Ainsley had thought living closer to the city would be easier on us all, especially when life started to get busier with the kids' extracurriculars and our jobs. When I'd found the listing for this plot of land, I'd fallen in love with it. It was our own little oasis. All the privacy we could ever need and still just a few minutes from everything.

Of course, now that I was alone out here, what had once felt like an oasis now felt like the prison walls were closing in.

You could go crazy out there in the woods alone.

I was beginning to understand that.

I wasn't built to be alone.

Know your strengths and all that...

I needed my wife back. I needed my kids back.

I needed the chaos and craziness that came with them being home.

It hurt that the kids weren't answering my calls or texts, even just to say hello or that they missed me as much as I missed them. I'd never gone so long without talking to them, which meant there had to be a reason. I could only imagine what horrible lies she'd fed them about me, but soon enough, I'd let them know the truth.

As I drove down the long driveway, I glanced out my window, seeing the trees zipping past and remembering the way the boys used to meet me at the end of the driveway when I'd arrive home and race the car with their bikes.

I remembered how excited they'd get when we'd see a deer in the woods. And how we'd take hikes on particularly nice days in the summer.

So much had changed over the course of the years, and I'd never really stopped to examine the why of it all, but now, I was beginning to understand it.

Ainsley had become so preoccupied with fixing us all, she'd let everything else fall by the wayside. We weren't her projects, but you could never convince her of that.

As much as I loved my wife, I'd enabled her to become what she was, and now, I was paying the consequences.

My children were paying the consequences.

Farther into town, I pulled into a store's parking lot

and stopped the car. Inside the store, I moved down the aisles with purpose, seeking out some of the kids' favorite things. For Maisy, I picked up three novels from the very limited young adult section. For Dylan, I found his favorite cologne, a book on one of his favorite musicians, and the expensive pomade he loved but rarely got. Riley was last and maybe the easiest—two bags of chips and a Harry Potter LEGO set I was pretty sure he didn't already own.

With all of the kids' gifts in the cart, I began to fret over what would bring Ainsley home. Would a gift be enough? An apology? What would convince her I forgave her enough to bring her home to me? I kept waiting for the phone to ring again—I wouldn't be the one to call her, but if she called again, I just might answer.

I'd hoped she'd leave a voicemail, but no such luck.

Moving down the next aisle, I smelled perfumes and creams, deciding on a bath salt scrub I knew she loved and then moved to the women's clothing. The hot-pink robe she loved so much had been destroyed in the fire, so I picked out a similar one and tossed it into the cart. If that wasn't enough, I wasn't sure what was. After all, she was the one who should be apologizing. *She* should be buying *me* gifts.

But this was just the kind of man I was.

Always giving.

Always thoughtful.

My wife was so lucky.

CHAPTER THIRTEEN

AINSLEY

C hecking into a hotel with cash was, apparently, not as easy as they make it appear on television. Despite the fact that I was willing to pay for the entire stay up front, the hotel required a card to be put on file.

"You're sure this won't end up on my statement at all?" I asked, for what must've been the third or fourth time. The woman behind the counter, whose name tag told me her name was Heather, didn't meet my eye as she answered.

"I assure you, ma'am, unless there are damages, we won't need to charge your card. You've put the cash deposit down for incidentals, so you're covered. It's just policy." She looked up finally, making eye contact with each of the kids, and then me. "Is there anything else I can do for you?"

"No." I tapped the room key on the counter and stepped back. "Thank you."

"Your elevator is this way." She pointed down the hall to her right, turning back to the book she'd placed facedown and open on the counter when we walked in.

I led the kids toward the elevator, checking over my shoulder every few moments to be sure they were with me and we weren't being followed. I knew my husband, and I knew what he was capable of under normal circumstances, but when fearing him, he'd suddenly turned into a supervillain in my mind.

I worried he'd bugged every room or building I entered. I worried he could disguise himself as everyone I passed. I worried he'd hacked my phone to track my location. It was maddening, not knowing where he was or what his next move would be. I considered calling him again, but if the last call was any indication, I assumed he wouldn't answer.

The room we checked into was small and smelled vaguely of stale cigarette smoke despite it being a nonsmoking room. "Don't put your bags on the floor," I warned, when Riley dropped his next to the bed. "Germs." They followed my lead, placing their bags next to mine on the desk on the far side of the room.

I spun around, my eyes traveling the room—the bright-white comforter and padded headboard, the mysteriously stained carpet, the raised water rings on the television stand. It wasn't the nicest hotel I'd ever stayed at—far from it, in fact—but it was somewhere we could stay for quite a while with the cash I'd withdrawn, and that was what I needed.

"Alright, I need a shower. What do you guys want to do tonight? Should we order pizza?"

"I want to go home, Mom. That's what I want to do tonight." I turned to face my son, surprised by the harshness of his tone. Dylan stared at me, his jaw tight. He looked so much like his father at that moment it brought tears to my eyes. He gestured toward Riley at his side. "We all do."

I released a puff of air, sinking down onto the bed behind me. "I know, guys. I know." I pinched the bridge of my nose, squeezing my eyes shut to stave off the migraine I could feel forming. "Look, I've been trying to avoid this, but..." I patted the bed next to me finally. There was no use trying to lie anymore. They needed to know something. I couldn't keep hiding it all from them. This wasn't the arrangement anymore. They deserved to know as much as I could tell them. "It's time I told you all what's going on."

Maisy sat down beside me. Her features were so childlike, maybe more than I'd noticed in so long. She was still a child. A baby. How could I ever tell her the truth about the horrors her parents had caused?

Dylan and Riley took a seat opposite us, their stances and expressions so similar it was getting hard to tell them apart.

"We can handle it." Dylan's voice was low. He thought he was prepared for anything.

"Your father and I are taking some time apart." I'd never uttered anything as painful as that sentence. I watched the weight of it wash over my children, as real as if I'd told them someone had died. I guess, in a way, someone had. The family we'd once been would never be whole again. "I'm sorry to tell you this way. I wanted to handle it so much better than this. But I can't keep hiding it from you anymore." I rubbed Maisy's back as she stared at me, her expression vacant and haunted.

"So...you're getting a divorce?" Riley asked, looking to his brother for assurance.

"Well, we haven't made any decisions," I offered. Then, not wanting to give them false hope, I added, "But, yes. Most likely, we're going to be getting a divorce."

"Why?" Maisy's question was barely audible, a breath more than a word.

"Well, it's...complicated. But I guess the simplest answer is that we both want different things right now." Looking for guidance, I tried to replay every divorce conversation I'd ever seen on TV, any of which would be better than the divorce conversation I'd had with my mother as I watched my dad disappear down the driveway without a goodbye. *He's decided he doesn't love us anymore,* she'd said, simple as that. It was the only discussion we'd ever had about the subject, and it wasn't until years later I found out it was my mother's affair that had caused their marriage to unravel.

"The most important thing is that you understand how much your daddy and I love you. Because we both love the three of you so, so much. And none of this is your fault. We've just grown apart and...we tried to fix it every way we knew how, but it didn't work. Nothing worked. And sometimes..." I didn't realize I was crying until I felt the tear trailing down my cheek. I brushed it away quickly. "Sometimes things just don't work out. Sometimes people are more broken together than they could ever be apart."

"But if you still love each other...there has to be a way." Glimmering tears trailed down Maisy's pink cheeks.

"There's not, honey. I wish there was, I really do."

"So what does that mean?" Dylan asked. He was trying to be strong, maybe for his siblings, maybe for me. His voice was steady, cheeks pale, jaw locked tight. His hands formed fists in his lap. "What happens to us?"

"Well, what do you mean? Nothing happens to you."

"Who will we live with? Do we get to decide?"

The question was a knife to my gut. From what I'd read in my late-night doom scrolling, they were old enough...what if they *did* get to decide? What if they chose Peter? What if—despite doing everything I'd done to protect my kids—what if I lost them anyway? What if I lost them because they chose to leave me?

I swallowed, dusting away another tear. "Is that, um, is that what you want?"

Dylan was slow to answer, not meeting my eyes. "I want to talk to Dad."

"You will," I promised. "You'll get to. But right now, he's away on a project, and we agreed it would be best if you stayed with me for the time being."

"So, why are we here, then?" he asked. "Why can't we go home?"

"We will. We're just sorting a few things out."

"It feels like we're hiding."

"We're not hiding," I lied. Now *I* couldn't meet *his* eye.

"Can we talk to him? I've been trying to call him, but he isn't answering," Dylan said, lifting his phone and staring at the screen. I nodded, relieved that I'd had the forethought to block their father's numbers from their phones and block the children's numbers from his before we'd left for Florida. At the time, it had seemed silly. Just one more scenario for me to overthink. But now, I was incredibly grateful I'd taken the time to do it.

I forced a smile, unwilling to let the hurt I felt over the attempts to contact his father outweigh my relief that he couldn't. "He's working on a project in the mountains, and I don't think he has great service. I'm sure he'll call you as soon as he can."

"What if he doesn't?" He stood from the bed.

"What do you mean?"

"What if he doesn't call? What if he doesn't want to talk to us?" He couldn't stop the tears that fell then, or the way his voice cracked as he asked the final question.

"Oh, sweetheart." I stood, reaching out my arms for him, but he backed away.

"Just don't."

I dropped my arms, nodding slowly. "Dylan, your father would do anything to be here with you right now. You know that. We wanted to tell you together. He wanted to be here for you. This is... I know how hard it is for you, guys. Believe me, I do. It's the last thing we ever wanted to do. I know how much it hurts—"

"Oh, save it, Mom—"

"I do. I know. I remember. We did everything we could to prevent this. I did everything I could—"

"Not everything, obviously," he said with a shrug. "Because here we are. And, what do you know? It hurts all the same." With that, he strutted toward the door and jerked it open.

"Dylan, wait—"

He turned back around, the door still open. "You know, you say you know what this feels like, but if that's true...you'd have to be the most selfish person on the planet to do it anyway."

His words sucked the air from my lungs. I took a step back, bitter tears burning my eyes. I was powerless to stop him from leaving the room, to stop him from leaving me.

Just like I'd been powerless to stop Peter.

A hand on my back caused me to jolt, and I looked over, realizing Riley was standing next to me. His smile was small and sad, and I wanted to bundle him up and take all the pain away from him. From all of them.

"I'm so sorry, bud." I dropped to my knees and let his head rest on my shoulder, no longer worried about the filthy carpet as I wrapped my arms around him, comforting his silent tears. "I'm so sorry."

I heard the bed shift under Maisy's weight and felt her hand in my hair. They were comforting me as much as I was comforting them at that moment. When I looked up, she rested her head on my opposite shoulder, hugging me back.

"It's all going to be okay," I vowed. "I know it doesn't feel like it right now, but I promise you, it's all going to be okay."

Somehow, someway, I'd make sure that was true.

CHAPTER FOURTEEN

PETER

I parked at the end of the cul-de-sac where Adele lived, watching the house for Ainsley and the kids carefully. Every time a curtain moved or a light switched on, my chest filled with hope, only to be let down when I caught a glimpse of my mother-in-law rather than my wife or kids.

As the cul-de-sac grew dark, I began to notice strange looks from neighbors walking their dogs or bringing out their garbage cans. When a porch light at the house I was parked in front of flicked on and a man and woman appeared in the illuminated doorway, staring at me and talking among themselves, I started to worry about what they might do. If they called the cops, how would I explain this?

Sorry, Officer, my wife tried to kill me and took off with my kids, so I'm just trying to track her down. Not to worry. Have a great night.

My fears weren't justified, though. It seemed they

had no intention of calling the police and were much more the type to handle things themselves when the man —a beefy guy with a thick neck and no shirt to cover the dark hair on his chest—lumbered toward my car. I avoided eye contact, pressing the phone to my ear as if I were talking on it. My heart thudded in my ears as he grew closer.

And closer.

And closer.

Bang.

Bang.

Bang.

"Can I help you, buddy?" he shouted through the thick pane of glass separating us.

I didn't dare roll down my window. "Excuse me?" I pulled the phone away from my ear, covering the screen with my hand as if he'd interrupted my imaginary phone conversation.

"Why are you sitting outside my house? You've been here all afternoon and evening. You spyin' on us or somethin'?"

"Spying?" I scoffed. "No. I don't even know you. I'm waiting for someone."

"Well, wait for 'em somewhere else, before I call the cops."

"It's a public street," I said, shaking my head, but I started the car anyway.

"Public street down there, too. Get outta here." He walked away, waving an angry hand over his head and mumbling to himself. The woman was still watching me cautiously, moths buzzing around her head in the porch light.

I eased the car forward slowly, trying to decide my next move. I wanted to stay and wait for Ainsley to return, but a huge part of me felt like I already knew she wasn't coming back.

Likely, I'd spooked her by showing up and talking to Adele. If Adele had warned her...

I'd known it was a risk leaving when Adele sent me away, but I didn't have a choice. Though I was still in the rental car, if Ainsley saw any strange car there, she wouldn't have come home. If she recognized me, she would've driven away, and then I really would've lost her.

Now, if I had any hope of her coming back at all, I needed to make her think I was giving up. I needed her to trust that I believed she wasn't there.

I eyed the grocery sack in the seat beside me.

If she could only see how hard I was trying.

I pulled out of the subdivision and along the street in front of a house that looked empty, digging my phone from my pocket.

I dialed Dylan's number, listening to it ring four times before going to voicemail. Why did he hate me? What had she done? What sort of poison was Ainsley giving the children about me? What sort of lies would make them ignore their own father's phone calls?

Whatever they were, I had secrets of my own I could share with them, if that's how she wanted to play.

I'd thought we were better than that, but with every unanswered call or text, I was beginning to see that wasn't the case. I wouldn't have my children hating me, even if that meant turning them against their mother.

Even if that meant bringing her down in a way I desperately didn't want to do. Once, Ainsley had fought for us in a way that had changed everything. If it came to it, I would be willing to do the same this time.

I pulled up the banking app on my phone and logged into our account, hoping—but not counting on the fact—that she'd have used the card somewhere that might give me a hint of where she might be. I didn't assume my wife was foolish enough to put another hotel on our debit card, now that she knew I was looking for her, and I'd put a freeze on our two other credit cards, hoping to narrow down the places I'd have to search. Our main credit card was nearly maxed out from the rental car payments.

Speaking of which, I'd need to make a payment soon, if I could figure out how.

Ainsley had always taken care of that sort of thing.

When the app loaded, I stared at the screen with horror, a chilling sensation in my core.

What the...

It wasn't possible.

She wouldn't.

Oh, who was I kidding? There was no use trying to fool myself anymore. No use pretending she wasn't exactly who she'd shown herself to be.

A selfish monster.

There was nothing my wife wouldn't do to protect herself. I'd learned that the hard way, but still, I hadn't seen this coming. She'd taken everything. We were left with just a hundred dollars between all four accounts, not even enough to cover the rental car fee, which I'd have to return sooner than I'd planned. And now, she'd disappeared, too.

So, maybe I'd have to take more drastic measures than I'd realized.

CHAPTER FIFTEEN

AINSLEY

When I finally found Dylan, he was sitting on one of the plastic lawn chairs around the indoor pool. The humidity of the room struck me as I opened the door, causing sweat to bead on my forehead in seconds. He looked up, as if surprised to see me, then back down, purposefully avoiding eye contact.

I walked toward him slowly, chin tucked, and sat down on the long seat of the lounge chair next to him. The plastic straps groaned under my weight, their once white material now yellowed and dry-rotting.

His arms were folded across his chest, head turned so he couldn't be tempted to look at me.

"When my dad left," I said, preparing to tell a story I'd never told anyone in my life, "I blamed myself. I thought there had to be something I could do to fix whatever it was that had gone wrong. I thought because I was part of the family, I had to have had some role in why things fell apart for them."

"Spare me the pity party. I'm not blaming myself. I'm blaming you."

"You should."

That seemed to surprise him. His eyes darted to meet mine. "Huh?"

"You *should* blame me, Dylan. That's exactly my point. Everything that's happened...it's because of me."

His hands went to his sides and he pushed himself up slightly, adjusting in his seat. "I don't understand."

"Dylan, sweetheart, marriage is...complicated, okay? But the truth is, if we wanted to stay together, your father and I, I'm sure we could."

"Is this supposed to make me feel better?"

"We could stay together and work through our problems and be a family for you kids. And, for a long time, that's what I wanted." I closed my eyes, looking down. "That's all I wanted. But we tried. We fought for our marriage. Because we love each other and because we love you."

"But if you love each other—"

"There are some things that love can't fix. I didn't want to admit that, even to myself, because I like to think I can fix anything." I smiled, hoping to get even a hint of a grin from him, but it didn't work. "But no matter what we did, we just couldn't get it right between the two of us. And then I started to think...what if you, or your brother or your sister, were in a marriage like this? What if you weren't happy?" I cocked my head to the side, willing him to understand. "And the truth is...if any of you came to me and told me you felt the way I feel... I'd tell you to walk away, to burn it all down, and to do whatever it takes to make yourself happy."

"So that's what this is? Consequences be damned?"

I winced at his harsh language, but fought the urge to chide him. "No. It's not about that. The truth is, even though I know I can be happier outside of this marriage, I would stay for you guys. I would stay to keep you happy and healthy and feeling whole."

"So do that." He unfolded and refolded his arms, a glint of hope in his eyes.

"But...if I did that I would be showing you three that your own happiness doesn't matter. And then, if you ever came to me in a similar situation, I'd be a hypocrite to tell you to leave. As much as it sucks, bud, I have to lead by example. Because I want you all to have an idea of what a whole, happy person is supposed to look like. And, maybe you can't understand that. Maybe it's selfish of me to ask you to. I don't know. I'm still figuring all of this out right along with you. What I do know, though, is that I want to teach you all that you are whole people completely on your own, and that you should never stay in a situation where you don't feel loved and respected. And that isn't meant to speak ill of your dad. He is a good person and a good father, and he loves you all so much. But our marriage is not one I would want for you guys, and that tells me all I need to know."

I paused, hoping he'd say something—anything—to let me know he understood, but he was silent, staring at me as if I were a stranger. "I understand that it's a lot to take in. And I understand if you can't...forgive me or look at me right now. These next few days, weeks, and months are going to be rough on us all. But I'll be here if you have any questions."

He lifted his chin slightly, a challenge. "Can I go live with Dad?"

I swallowed, fighting back tears. "If that's what you want, we—"

"It is."

I stood. This was not about me. This was about him. I couldn't cry. He didn't deserve to see me cry. His feelings were valid.

"Okay, then. I'll, um, I'll see what I can do." I turned before the first tear fell and walked from the room with a slow, confident pace.

I thought no one could ever hurt me like Peter had.

I'd been wrong.

CHAPTER SIXTEEN

PETER

"Gin and tonic." I slapped a hand on the bar, debit card pinned between two fingers when the bartender finally turned to face me. Might as well use up the rest of the money before Ainsley stole that too.

"Sure thing, hon," she said, flicking her dark, curly hair over her shoulder so I had a clear view of the low-cut shirt she was wearing.

I waited for the familiar tingle of excitement to spread through my core, but to my surprise, nothing happened. I felt nothing at all.

She slid the drink to me, taking the card and handing me a receipt to sign moments later. When I turned away from the bar, a woman with long, red hair stood behind me. I did a double take at the sight of her, convinced, if only for a second, that it was Ainsley standing there.

To my disappointment, the girl was years younger than my wife, and the red of her hair was too bright—too fake. I hated her in an instant, as if she'd come there just to torment me. Just to remind me Ainsley was gone.

I shoved past her, my arm colliding with her shoulder with extra force.

"Hey, excuse you!" she shouted, spinning around as if ready to start a fight.

Her fire amused me.

"Excuse me." I smiled at her, my anger fading slightly. "Sorry, I was distracted. Are you okay?"

She simmered down, dropping to her flat feet from off her tiptoes. "Um, yeah. I am. It seemed like you did that on purpose or something. Sorry for yelling at you. It's been a weird day."

"For me, too," I admitted, then shot a look at the bartender behind her. "Can I make it up to you? Buy you a drink?"

"Oh, um." She eyed the folded cash in her hand, then shoved it back into her pocket. "What the hell. Why not?"

"Why not?" I repeated, stepping forward. "What'll it be?"

"I'll have a..." She scanned the row of alcohol behind the bartender, who appeared to only be half listening as she slid two bottles of beer toward the man next to us. "Manhattan, please. With Basil Hayden's and extra cherry juice."

The bartender set to work and the woman turned to me, smacking her gum with confidence. "You gotta name?"

"Last I checked it's Peter."

Last I checked? I fought back a grimace.

"Nikki," she said, reaching for the bowl of nuts in the center of the bar and taking a handful. I watched the man next to us eyeing her and stepped closer. He glanced at me, then back at her, and turned away.

"You come here often, Nikki?" I asked, my voice raised slightly as the song changed to something more up-tempo. I leaned in closer to hear her reply.

"Nah, I'm in town for a funeral."

I jerked my head back in shock at her answer. "No kidding?"

"Yep."

"I'm sorry for your loss."

"Eh, it wasn't that big of a loss." She blew a bubble and popped it loudly, outstretching her hand to take the drink as the bartender held it out. "Thanks."

I paid for her drink and then we moved through the crowd quickly, finding an empty booth in the far corner of the room. She sat down first, not expecting or allowing me to sit next to her. I slid onto the opposite bench.

"So, what do you do, Peter?"

"I'm an architect."

That earned me a look of approval. One I was very familiar with. She grinned, leaning in to take a sip of her drink. When the drink touched her lips, she spit it out, covering her mouth as her cheeks turned pink with embarrassment.

"Oh my god, that's awful," she said, her face wrinkled with disgust. She fanned her tongue with her hands, laughing in spite of herself. "I'm so sorry. I thought I would seem sophisticated ordering a drink I heard my ex order once. But..." She fought to keep herself from gagging. "Oh, it's so bad. Why didn't anybody tell me it was so bad?"

The tension left my shoulders. "It's the bitters. Not a drink for everyone."

She pushed it away, a bit of the dark liquid sloshing out onto the table. "You aren't kidding. I'll be right back."

She stood, scurrying across the room and back to the bar. I pulled the drink closer to me and out of the way, wondering if she'd gotten enough of the drug in her system to have any effect.

Probably not was my guess.

Moments later, she returned with a colorful cocktail in a glass, looking pleased with herself.

"Well, now that I've completely embarrassed myself, let's start over. Hi, Peter the architect. I'm Nikki, the full-time student, part-time nanny." She held out her hand, shaking mine with mock sincerity.

So, she was actually as young as she looked.

Consider me curious.

"What are you going to school for?" I swirled the stirrer in my drink, the trill of the ice in my glass almost hypnotizing.

"Culinary arts, actually," she said, as if it were something impressive. "I want to open my own cupcake bakery."

"Just cupcakes?"

"Mhm." She gave a proud nod. "*Just* cupcakes. Actually, that's what I want to call it."

"Well, it would certainly cut down on confusion." Her expression changed, cooling slightly as she seemed to realize I was making fun of her, so I added, "Hey, who doesn't love cupcakes? Sounds like a good idea to me."

She giggled, rubbing her hands together. "So, tell me more about yourself. Do you live in Nashville?"

I shook my head quickly, used to lying my way through this question. "No. I'm just in town for business."

"Oh, interesting." She twirled her straw, not sounding the least bit interested. "Do you have a girlfriend?"

"No." It wasn't a lie. A wife wasn't a girlfriend. "I wouldn't be sitting here talking to you if I did, now would I?"

"You'd be surprised."

I sighed, resting an arm on the back of the booth. "Yeah, there are a lot of creeps out there."

"I can't tell if you're joking, but there really are. It's tough being a woman these days."

"I get it." I took another drink.

God, she was annoying.

Why did I care?

Why was I suffering through this?

If I asked her to leave with me right now, I was sure she would, even without the coercion of the drug I'd placed in her wasted drink. So, why couldn't I ask her?

It wasn't that she wasn't attractive enough—I never cared about that.

It certainly wasn't that she wasn't annoying me enough.

Something was stopping me. A block of some sort.

Suddenly it hit me... I couldn't bring myself to *want* to do it. It sounded about as fun as washing the car or painting the house. And it was a hell of a lot more work.

I wasn't interested, not only in her, but in any of the women in the bar. Not because of some sudden change of heart, but more out of what felt like...laziness? Apathy?

I didn't care about the girl. Didn't care about the chase.

Ordinarily, the things I had planned for her were the only things that brought me clarity on my darkest days, but tonight...tonight I couldn't do it.

"I love this song," she squealed as the music changed to something else I didn't recognize. "Do you know it?"

I cocked my ear to the side, as if I were trying to listen. "I don't think so."

If I took her home with me, if I just forced myself back into old habits, it would take my mind off of everything wrong with my life.

I could do it. It would be easy. And, once I'd started, I wouldn't be able to stop.

"Hey, do you want to get out of here?" I asked, leaning forward and slurping down the rest of my drink. The alcohol burned my throat.

She smiled, running a finger around the rim of her glass. "Well, I want to finish my drink first. And...maybe have another." She batted her eyelashes at me, and I pictured bashing her skull in. I could practically smell the blood.

But I didn't want to.

As real as the possibility was, I just...didn't want to.

God, what was wrong with me?

I slid out of the booth without warning. "I've gotta go."

"Wait, what? I was just kidding." She reached for my hand, and her skin on mine repulsed me. I felt like one of those guys who gets hypnotized to make their cigarettes taste like worms.

Everything I'd ever loved, everything I'd ever craved... felt pointless.

Unappealing.

Disgusting, even.

I couldn't have been less into it.

"No, it's fine. I just remembered I have to..." I didn't bother finishing the sentence, already making my way across the bar and toward the front door.

What was wrong with me?

What had Ainsley done?

CHAPTER SEVENTEEN

AINSLEY

It was after eleven before Dylan finally returned to the room. Maisy and Riley were already asleep, and I pointed toward the box of pizza resting on top of the mini-fridge when he looked at me.

"We got your favorite."

He walked past the pizza box without a word, kicking off his shoes and sliding into bed next to Riley. He pulled the covers up over his shoulders. I considered reminding him to brush his teeth, but thought better of it.

"Love you," I whispered, to no response.

I watched him, waiting for him to look my way, to offer me even a moment's glance to let me know the hatred didn't run too deep, but it never came. I couldn't blame him.

I *did* know how it felt.

I was glad he had at least one parent who was there for him, but I knew that didn't make it better. Going through my parents' divorce was the most isolating experience of my life, and I knew each of the kids would have to work through it in their own ways and their own time, no matter how badly it stung. What I knew most of all was that I couldn't allow him to get in touch with Peter. I couldn't allow Peter to get to him. If I did, I worried I'd never see my son again.

When an hour had passed and the large lump in the bed that was my oldest son rose and fell with steady breaths, telling me he was asleep, I picked up my phone.

She answered on the first ring, as if she'd been expecting my call. Maybe she had. She always seemed to sense when I needed her.

"Hey, love. Whatcha up to?"

"Oh, you know..." Just the sound of Glennon's voice put me at ease. "Just sitting here watching TV."

"Anything good?"

"Not really. What are you up to?"

"I was reading the new Brené Brown book. Have you read it yet? Life changing."

"I wouldn't expect anything less."

"Everything okay? You sound sad."

"Hm? Oh, yeah, I'm fine. I just... I need a favor."

"Okay. What's going on?"

I cleared my throat. "I, um, well... Where are you right now?"

"We're in Boulder for the next three and a half weeks, why? Is everything okay?"

Try as I might, I couldn't decide how to bring it up. Saying the words aloud made them real, and I desperately didn't want them to be real. "I was hoping that you might be down for some visitors."

"What? Seriously? Of course I am. Always. That would be amazing. We *are* talking about you guys, right?" She laughed. "I should probably clarify before getting ahead of myself."

"It would just be the kids. I can get them a plane ticket to Denver first thing in the morning. I need them to stay with you for a few days. Is that okay?"

She hesitated. "Of course it's okay, but...is something going on? Haven't they started school?"

"I convinced the school to give them extra time off around fall break for an educational trip. They just have to turn in papers about it. We went to a museum and an aquarium in Florida."

"You were in Florida? Are you in Florida now?"

"No, we're...actually, we're at a hotel in Nashville."

"Oooh, a hotel? Fun. A little staycation or something? Are you and Peter getting some alone time?"

I sucked in a sharp breath, tucking my shaking hand under my leg. "Actually, Peter and I are splitting up."

"Oh, babe... I'm—gosh, I'm so sorry. I know you'd been having problems before, but I really thought you seemed better."

"We were. We were better until we became worse. And now—" I stood, turning to face the window if only so I didn't have to look at my children as I said it. "Now, I don't see a way forward. He's... He's lied to me, Glennon. For so long—"

"About what? About Seth?" She was moving around

on her end—the gentle swish of air into the microphone enough to tell me she was trying to get away from present company.

"No. No, it's not about Seth. It's about, well, everything. There's so much I haven't told you lately, and I can't get into it right now, not over the phone." Glancing over my shoulder at my children, I lowered my voice again. "I just need you to take the kids so I can be sure they're safe and taken care of."

She was serious then, her voice low. "Of course. Babe, whatever I can do, just name it."

"If I put them on a flight to Denver, you'll pick them up?"

"Of course," she assured me again. "But...won't you come, too? It sounds like you could use—"

"I can't. Not yet. I promise I will. And I promise I'll explain everything as soon as I can. Right now, though, I have things I still need to take care of here."

She released a long breath. "You swear to me you're not going to do anything stupid or dangerous, right?"

"You know me better than that."

A beat passed, both of us silent, and then she said, somewhat begrudgingly, "I never should've left you for this long. I told Seth you still needed me."

"Glennon, no. This isn't your fault. I'm a big girl, okay? I can handle myself. Everything's going to be fine, I promise you."

I heard a man's voice in the background say something soft and low. Her hand swiped across the speaker as she responded. "Be right there."

"That doesn't sound like Seth."

When she returned to our conversation, she said, "It wasn't. I'm...on a date."

"You *what?* You're on a date? What are you doing talking to me?" My jaw dropped.

"Stop," she said firmly, without time or patience for my nonsense. "Family first, babe. And you're family."

"I'm sorry..." I whispered, but sorry for what, I still wasn't sure. Tears stung my eyes, the weight of the apology hanging in the air.

"There's no reason to be."

I swiped a tear from my cheek, steadying my voice before I spoke again. "I'll, uh, I'll get the flight information sent over to you. And I'll call you in the morning to set it all up, okay?"

"Okay." Her tone was soft as she waited for me to say more, but I couldn't.

"Now, go enjoy the rest of your date. I'll be fine, I promise. I *am* fine."

"I can talk as long as you need. He's still fixing dinner and—"

"I'm fine," I swore again, forcing my tone to be more convincing. "Honestly. Go, have fun. I need to look at flights before I pass out. It's been a long day."

"If you're sure..."

"Positive."

"Okay. Love you, babe."

"Love you. Talk soon."

I ended the call just as more tears began to fall. My best friend was moving on, as she should. My husband wanted to kill me. My mother thought I should stay with him anyway. My kids hated me.

I was alone.

And with good reason.

I deserved to be alone after all I'd done.

But not until I made Peter pay.

CHAPTER EIGHTEEN

PETER

I drove through the town that night without direction. Turning down side streets and taking curves too fast. I needed to move, to act, to do something, but there was nothing to do. Ainsley had slipped through my fingers. She was gone, maybe for good, and she'd ruined me with her departure.

She'd taken away from me the one thing I'd ever been good at.

My knuckles throbbed from where I'd pounded them against the steering wheel while sitting outside of the bar.

What was I becoming? What had I let her turn me into? Why did I even care?

Think...

Think...

Think...

I needed to get inside of her head. It wouldn't be easy. She'd spent our entire marriage inside of mine, so even if I tried to think like her, she'd probably predict it and still manage to stay a step ahead of me. But there had to be a way. I knew her. I knew what she ate and what perfume she wore; I knew what made her feel better when she was sick and how she looked when she was sleeping.

I knew her.

Maybe better than anyone else, but still. My wife was an impenetrable wall, without gates or scaffolding for anyone. Whatever I knew about her, it was merely what she'd let me know.

Let me believe.

A sudden thought hit me, and I pulled the SUV over to the shoulder in an instant.

I was wrong.

I did know something.

Something important.

Lifting my phone from where it rested in the center console, I opened my call log and clicked on her name, then waited. I was breaking my promise to myself, but I didn't care. This was more important.

"Hello?"

I was silent, thinking I'd somehow imagined it. I never expected her to actually answer. I'd been preparing to leave her a voicemail, one I knew she'd have to respond to, but this... I didn't know how to—

"Hello?" She sounded impatient.

"Ainsley?"

"Who else would it be?"

"I didn't think you'd answer."

"At least one of us can answer the phone. We should meet."

Now I was convinced I was dreaming. "I couldn't agree more."

"When?"

"Now. I'll come to you. Where are you?"

"That doesn't work for me."

There was the woman I knew. "Well, gosh, when can you pencil me in?"

"Tomorrow. Ten a.m."

"Where?"

"The house."

"Fine." I fought against the urge to mention that I knew she'd stolen our money. I needed her to show up, after all. I had to be civilized. "You good?"

She was quiet for a moment, so quiet I thought she was going to hang up, but then she said, "Did you just ask if I'm *good?*"

"Yeah, I just... I miss you. I miss the kids. Are you all okay?"

"Don't make this something it isn't, Peter. I'm meeting you because there are things we need to discuss, that's it."

"How am I *making* this anything? I'm just checking on you."

"You don't need to do that."

"Fine. I won't."

"I'll see you in the morning."

I sucked in a sharp breath, casting a line of hope. "Bring the kids. Please."

"I won't be doing that."

I hadn't expected any different, but I had to ask. "Fine. Just...tell them I miss them, okay?"

"Goodbye, Peter."

"Hey, Ains, *wait!*"

She paused for a beat. "Yeah?"

"Um, thanks for...for answering."

"You're welcome." With that, the line beeped, alerting me that the call had ended and she was gone. My heart raced as if I'd run a marathon; a thin sheen of sweat soaked my skin.

It was happening.

I was finally going to see her.

I was finally going to take care of everything, once and for all.

THE NEXT MORNING, I was standing outside the house, pacing and listening intently for any sign of her. When I finally heard her car pulling down the driveway five minutes after ten, I got into position, hiding in the shadows just inside the frame of the garage's side door.

My breathing was shallow as the car door slammed shut. Her shoes crunched against the gravel drive. Would she have worn heels that could pierce my skin with a swift kick? Or sensible shoes for running away?

I imagined she'd brought a weapon of some sort. A knife, most likely. Definitely not a gun. Maybe the old bat she'd been hiding—I wasn't entirely convinced she'd disposed of it like she promised.

Crunch.

Breathe.

Crunch.

Breathe.

Crunch.

Breathe.

The crunching steps were silenced when she stepped onto the concrete walkway that led to the porch. She was going to walk right past me. I held my breath, focusing intently on the silence.

Where are you, Ains?

She stepped into my view, stopping just a few feet from the porch, and scanned the yard, searching for me. She had no idea how close I was. Hidden in the shadows. Lurking. Looming.

I waited as she took another step.

Then another.

Then another.

She was past me, heading for the porch.

Now.

"*Hey—*" I stepped forward. She spun around, obviously expecting me. Her arm shot out, wielding a weapon I couldn't see. My body jolted as white-hot lightning shot through my core. My vision blurred, black splotches painting through a sea of white. I doubled over, the pain so intense I was sure I was going to vomit. The sound came again—like packaging tape being ripped from the roll...only more electric, more intense. I couldn't open my jaw. Couldn't breathe. Couldn't move.

"Step back," Ainsley said, shoving the weapon into my stomach harder. The sound stopped in an instant, the bright light in her hand dimming.

I fumbled backward into the garage, reaching for the wall to steady myself. She followed close behind. "What the..." I panted, touching the place where I'd been convinced only moments ago that she'd stabbed me. "You...*tased* me?"

She eyed the pink contraption in her hand with an unimpressed expression. "It's a stun gun. Don't be ridiculous."

"Is there a difference?" I put my hands up to stop her from moving near me, trying to catch my breath. We were repelling magnets. For every step she took toward me, I took a step away.

"Is that really what you want to talk about right now? The difference between stun guns and Tasers?"

I winced as I took another step backward, bumping into my SUV. The garage was cluttered, without much room to maneuver, even without her car in its usual parking space. I eyed the button on the wall that would lift the overhead doors, giving us fresh air and me a way to escape, but if I moved, she'd come after me again. It wasn't an option. "You didn't have to do that. I wasn't going to hurt you." I held my hands out in the air. "I'm unarmed."

"Yeah, well, you'll forgive me if I don't believe you."

"Hey, you're the one who tried to kill me, if memory serves."

She smirked—*she actually smirked*—as the memory danced across her face, a whimsical look in her eyes. In a flash, it was gone. Wiped away so fast I could almost be convinced I hadn't seen it at all. She stared at me, her eyes cold and lifeless.

Who was she?

Most days, I didn't know.

Then again, how well do we ever know the people in our lives? How well can you know your spouse? Was there anyone out there who could say they'd never been surprised or disappointed by the person they loved most? Surely, we weren't the outliers. It was human nature. I had to believe everyone had parts of themselves they refused to display to anyone—the whispered motivations, internal desires, embarrassing decisions, and mortifying reasons behind actions we'd never dare reveal to anyone.

Still, I knew my wife as much as anyone could. And I was learning more about her every day.

I put a hand up, offering an apology before she asked for one. "I'm sorry. I'm, look, I'm not going to hurt you. I just want to talk. I was hoping you'd bring the kids."

"I told you I wouldn't, so I'm not sure why you'd hope that. The kids don't need to be here." She kept the stun gun held out between us—a constant warning.

"Fair enough. Well, I'm glad you came anyway."

She nodded. "I'm surprised to hear you say that." Her arms folded up, crossing over her chest, the weapon still clutched in her palm.

"I never wanted to hurt you, Ainsley. I only wanted to find you and apologize."

Her head drew back quickly. "Apologize?"

My muscles went weak, and I stepped toward her, though it was her turn to move back. "You were right about everything."

"I know that."

"I know, but I want you to hear me say it." I spoke the next words slowly, enunciating each syllable as if to prove the point. I needed her to hear me—really hear me—and understand. *"You were right about everything. I was stupid. I had everything in the world I could ever want handed to me on a silver platter, and it still wasn't enough. I was everything I hate in a person. In a husband. You're...you're it for me. I love you, Ainsley. I love you so damn much I can't think about anything else. And I know I screwed things up—I really, really do—but trust me when I say I've learned my lesson, I—"

"Learned your lesson?" She looked away from me, rolling her eyes. "Peter, you haven't begun to learn your lesson."

"Haven't begu— You tried to *kill me,* for Christ's sake. You sedated me. Left me to die in a fire which I *barely* escaped to put out, by the way. You *left me to die,* Ainsley. And tried to turn me in. You were going to make me look like a monster... After all we've been through. I know what I did was wrong. I know I hurt you. Everything with Joanna was...messy—"

"*Messy?* That's a nice way to describe it. I was giving you everything, Peter, doing everything I thought you wanted and you couldn't give me the time of day. Here I was, changing everything about myself for you and you had your precious little toy locked up in that room behind my back the whole time! You were so obsessed with her, so...so..."

"I got distracted," I admitted. "And I don't blame you for what you did. Killing her. I get it. It was the right thing to do. But I would've never hurt you. Never. Don't you see that?" I stepped toward her, keeping my voice steady and firm. In control. I wanted her to see that I had everything under control again.

"You *did* hurt me, Peter. Maybe not physically, but you just keep hurting me. That's why we're in this mess to begin with. And, anyway, that's not why I'm here." She unfolded and refolded her arms, glancing at the concrete floor under our feet.

"Well, why are you here, then?" I braced myself for what was to come, no idea what she might say.

"Because we have to figure out where we go from here. We need to call a truce."

"And I'm ready for that. I've told you... I want you to come home. Bring the kids. Let's fix this." I stepped toward her and she backed away again, but this time, she backed away with a look in her eyes that scared me. She wasn't retreating, she was restraining herself. A twinge of pain ran through my stomach, reminding me of the consequences of getting too close to her.

"I have no interest in fixing us, Peter. What was left of our marriage turned to ash in that house. I want nothing to do with you. Don't you get that?"

I tilted my head to the side slightly. "At the risk of getting tased again, I don't think that's true."

Her grimace faltered. "What do you mean?"

"I don't think you want to hurt me, Ainsley. I don't. I don't think you ever meant to."

"What the hell are you talking about? I tried to k—" She stopped, looking around. "Are you recording me? Is this some sort of setup?"

"Of course it isn't a setup." I scoffed, waving a hand around the garage.

She raised the stun gun to the space just in front of my neck. "Prove it."

I swallowed. "How would you like me to prove it?"

"Say you're a murderer."

"I'm a murderer," I repeated, keeping my eyes trained on the metal prongs in front of me.

"Say your name and what you've done."

"I'm Peter Greenburg. I've...I've killed loads of people. Women, mostly. Men too, lately." My eyes flicked up from the weapon to meet hers. "I'm a bad, bad man. Happy?"

She hesitated, but eventually lowered the pink weapon. Was its color meant to be so misleading? If you just saw it out of the corner of your eye, it could've been a makeup box or a bottle of perfume from her dresser.

With the weapon tucked safely back in her arms, she narrowed her gaze at me. "Make no mistake about it, Peter, I wanted to do much more than hurt you. If it wasn't for your little escape hatch, we wouldn't be having this conversation at all."

I clicked my tongue, my cheek drawing inward with smug disbelief. I couldn't help myself. I was beginning to feel sure I'd been right. "See, I don't think that's the case."

"What are you talking about?" she sneered.

"Ainsley, you're the most competent woman I know. You're always, always one step ahead of me. You fix things. You don't make mistakes. I've tried to think, but...I can't think of a single time where I recall you making a mistake. Not ever. You're...calculating. Meticulous. You think everything through ten ways to Sunday—"

"Six ways."

"What?"

"It's six ways to Sun..." she said halfheartedly. "Doesn't matter. What's your point?"

"My point is... Why would you mess up this *one* thing?" I held up a finger. "Probably the most important thing you've ever had to do? Why would you let even a tiny little possibility of me escaping slip under your radar?"

"I couldn't have known about the other door."

"But you still knew there might be a way. Why would you leave it to chance?" I studied her, watching for a confirmation in her eyes. Her chest rose and fell with heavy breaths. "You wouldn't," I filled in. "You wouldn't. Not if you actually wanted it done. If you wanted me to be dead, I'd be dead, Ainsley. There's no doubt in my mind. You killed Joanna. You killed Jim."

"It was different—"

"Because they meant nothing to you, and...because you love me."

Her eyes widened as if I'd slapped her. The tension in the room was thick, my words hanging in the air between us.

"You're delusional..." She stroked her arm as a means of self-comfort.

"If you wanted me dead, you wouldn't have knocked me out and set the house on fire and hoped for the best. You're too thorough for that. You'd have sliced my throat and watched me bleed out. You'd have checked for a pulse. You'd have buried me in the backyard and washed the blood off of every surface." I shook my head. "See, I've gone over it every way there is, and it just doesn't make sense. Unless—"

"You're insane, Peter. What you're saying is ridiculou—"

"Unless you didn't do it because you didn't actually want to kill me in the first place. You wanted to scare me. Punish me. Fair enough. But, honey, you don't leave anything to chance. You didn't kill me because...because you couldn't. Plain and simple. Because you didn't want me to die. Because..." I drew out the words, stepping closer to her. "Because...you...love...me."

I jolted again, my body on fire with electricity—true electricity—as she shoved the stun gun back into what felt like the exact same place on my stomach. The attack was quicker this time. Just a pulse.

"Don't flatter yourself, Peter. I didn't kill you because I needed to give the kids answers. If I buried you in the woods, I'd have to tell them you ran off somewhere. I needed a body. I needed a finale. I needed it to all be over."

"It isn't over, Ains. Don't you see that? We get to start fresh now. We get to fix this. And I don't care how many times you shock me"—I checked to be sure she wasn't planning to test that vow—"I'm not going anywhere. And I'm not changing my mind. Love me or kill me, those are your only options."

She was silent for a moment, then her jaw began to quiver. At first, I thought maybe she was going to start crying, but instead, I saw pure rage in her eyes. "You don't get to do that."

"I just did."

"No, Peter," she said, her voice a low growl. "No. *I'm leaving you.* I'm taking the kids. It is over. Do you hear me? It's over! We're done."

"We're not. You'll never be rid of me, don't you see that? We're made for each other, Ains. We're a perfect match. You can't leave me, not really. People who've been through everything we've been through together don't just get to walk away."

She bared her teeth, taking a step back from me. "I *am* leaving you. The kids are already gone, and I'm next. You'll never see us again. Don't contact us. Don't try to find us. Just move on with your life. Have the house—sell it, keep it, whatever. Have your secrets. Have your little hobbies. But we're done. *I'm* done."

"Wh-what are you talking about? Gone? Gone where? Where are the kids? Where are you going?"

"Are you even listening to me? I'm *not* telling you that—"

"But you can't just take them. I'm their father. They need me—"

"They need a murderer?" She charged toward me without warning, and I bumped into the car again in an attempt to back up. She wagged her finger at me, her nail practically scraping my nose. "A monster?"

"Pot meet kettle," I muttered. I hadn't meant to say it, but I couldn't help the slip.

"They don't need you," she repeated, her voice feral and ragged. She puffed out a breath, smoothing her shirt. "That's what I came here to say." Her eyes flitted back and forth between mine, as if she was searching for something—a question, an answer, a sign—and then she turned on her heel, prepared to leave me. I grabbed her arm without thinking, acting on pure animal instinct. She was going to take everything from me. She was going to leave me alone. She jerked back, ripping her arm from my grasp as if it were a fight for her life. "*Don't touch me,*" she shouted.

"Ainsley, please—"

"Don't ever touch me again," she said once more, her lips pressing into a thin line. She took another step back, holding the stun gun in the air as she reached the doorway. If I let her walk out, I'd never see her again.

I knew it in my gut.

If she escaped, that would be it. I'd have let her walk away from me without a fight. What would she do if the situation were reversed? What would she expect me to do?

"Why did you even come here?" I demanded. "If that was all you were going to tell me, why bother?"

"Because I needed you to *hear* it." She pointed at her ear. "Not consider it part of the chase. Not ignore me. I needed you to *hear* me say the words and see the absolute sincerity on my face. I needed to make sure you heard me loud and clear so there is no confusion."

I nodded slowly.

"Why are you smirking?"

Had I been?

"You wanted to see me."

She groaned, both hands near her temples. "You aren't listening to me."

"Oh, I'm listening just fine, but I know you better than you think I do, Ainsley. You wanted to see me. It's the only reason that makes sense for you coming here. I know that like I know you'd never actually take the kids away. Just like I know you're coming home. You'd never break up our family. You need us to be together. You need things to be normal."

"That's where you're wrong." She tucked a piece of hair behind her ear. "I'm not the same woman I was back then. I'm not the same woman you married. I've come to realize there are worse things than divorce. Worse things than breaking up a family. Much worse."

"I've been a good father to them."

"Debatable."

"How? Name one thing I've done to ever hurt—"

"How many times did you wash someone's blood from your hands in the same sink where your children brush their teeth at night?" She was growing frantic. "How many times have you missed things because you were so focused on someone chained up in your murder room?"

"I never use chains."

"How many times," she growled, "have you let your children down because you were too busy to notice that they needed you?"

"I could ask you the same thing."

She started to walk away, but stopped, spinning back to face me. "That's the difference between you and me, Peter. *I'm* willing to change. I *am* changing. You...you will never change." She looked me up and down, sizing me up with her upper lip curled in disgust.

"You're not even giving me a chance."

"I've given you thousands of chances. Years of chances. Eventually, it stops being your fault and starts being mine. I've enabled you and looked the other way for the sake of our family for far too long. But enough is enough. I deserve better. Your children deserve better."

"How do you think our children will feel when they find out you tried to kill me? When they find out you're the reason I'm not around?"

"They're never going to find out."

"I wouldn't be too sure about that."

"If you so much as attempt to contact them, Peter, I'll—"

"You'll what? What are you going to do?"

"I'll kill you again. And this time, I won't fail." She stopped, looking pleased with herself, and huffed out a breath. Then, she turned on her heel and hurried back outside and toward her car.

I rushed forward. I couldn't let her leave.

Wouldn't.

I grabbed hold of her. "Wait!"

She shoved me backward, pushing the stun gun into my chest. Her thumb missed the button, buying me a second's time. Without thinking, I smacked it from her hands, towering over her. I'd never once thought about hurting my wife, but something had flipped in me.

She couldn't leave.

I grabbed her arm again, jerking her toward me. She reared back, slapping my face with so much force my vision filled with black spots. I released her arm.

"I'm sorry... I..."

What was I thinking? I couldn't hurt her. I loved her. I needed her to believe that.

"Don't touch me!" she cried, backing away. She ran backward, keeping an eye on me as she moved, only spinning around when she reached her car.

"Please, can we just talk? This wasn't how I wanted today to go. Please, Ains—" I was just behind her, panting as I tried to keep up. She gripped the car door, and I narrowly missed it as she slammed it shut. She moved to lock the doors, but she wasn't fast enough.

I tore her door open. "Don't do this, Ainsley. Please. Please think about the kids. Please. I promise. I'll do whatever you want, I'll—"

It was no use. She put the car in reverse, backing the car up with a sudden jerk. The door handle was ripped from my grasp as she peeled away with the door swinging open. I jumped out of the way as she put the car in drive and sped away, gravel flying behind her. I watched her go, filled with hopeless frustration and powerlessness to stop her.

Was this really the end?

I couldn't believe it.

I couldn't let it be.

But what choice did I have?

CHAPTER NINETEEN

AINSLEY

I was several miles from the house before I stopped shaking. Several more miles away before I realized I was crying. The amount of adrenaline it had taken to face him again, to face my mistakes again, was enormous, and coming down from that high was painful and exhausting.

I drove in silence, checking the rearview mirror every few minutes for signs of him. I knew him better than to believe he was just going to let me go, though I hoped I was wrong. Peter was stubborn, almost as stubborn as I was, and determined.

I thought about what he'd said. Was he right about why I hadn't killed him myself? It was possible. As much as I hated him, as much as I wanted him out of my life, the idea of having his blood literally on my hands made me feel ill.

If he could just leave me alone, if we could just walk away from each other before someone else had to get hurt, wasn't that better? I had to believe so.

The sound of my phone ringing penetrated the silence, and I jumped, watching as the screen on the dashboard lit up to announce an incoming call.

I knew it was Peter without seeing the screen, which was why when I stared at my mother's name, I had to blink twice to be sure I wasn't seeing things.

"Mom?"

"Ainsley, where are you?"

"I'm...driving. Why?"

"Are you crying?" she asked, sounding distracted.

"No," I lied.

"You sound like you've been crying."

"I'm fine, Mom."

"Well, when is your flight?"

"Oh, I'm not sure. I haven't booked it yet."

"Why not? I thought that was why you needed my credit card number last night."

"No," I said simply. "Er, well, yes, it was. I used your card to load a prepaid visa, so we could book a flight when we're ready. Thank you again for letting me do that. I'll stop by your house this afternoon and bring the cash to pay you back for it."

"I still don't understand why you couldn't just pay for them from your own account. What's the deal with all this cash? Are you dealing drugs now? Is *that* why Peter left you?"

"No, Mom, I'm not dealing drugs." I rubbed the stress wrinkle from my forehead. "I told you, Peter and I decided to close the accounts in our name and open separate ones, in order to keep things civil while we figure out what we're doing. I just haven't had a chance to open my new one yet."

"I really think you're jumping the gun on this, Ainsley. It all seems very dramatic."

I bit my tongue, gripping the steering wheel until my knuckles turned white. "Yeah, well...it's done. Thanks again."

"*Wait*—" she cried, before I could hang up.

"What?"

"Come home," she said, then cleared her throat. "Come back to my house. I'm sorry for what I said. I'm sorry for not understanding. I just...let me help you."

"Mom, it's fine, honestly. I've got—"

"I'm not offering because I think you can't handle it. I know you better than that. I'm offering because you're my daughter. I may not always know the right thing to say, but that doesn't mean I don't want to...you know... It doesn't mean I don't care."

It was the closest I'd ever come to hearing my mother say she loved me.

"I've already paid for the hotel room. But I appreciate your offer. Really, I do."

She sighed. "Okay, well, do the kids need anything? Maybe I could order your dinner and have it delivered."

"No, I've got it covered. We're all fine. We have money and food, and we'll be out of here soon. I just had to take care of a few last-minute errands."

"Well, when will you be back?"

"I'm not sure," I lied again. "Maybe a few months."

"What about their school? And work? Will I see you at Thanksgiving?"

"Once we get where we're going, I'll enroll them in a new school. Or...homeschool. Maybe I'll do one of those online programs for the year. And, I'm still figuring out my work situation. I have no idea about any of the holidays. I'll let you know. It's all happening pretty quickly, and I can only take it one step at a time."

"Are you sure you wouldn't rather just stay with me?" she offered. "I can move my exercise equipment out of the spare room to give the kids a bedroom. They'd still be able to go to their schools, and you could go to work. It seems that would make the most sense."

"We have to get out of here, Mom. I can't...I can't stay here."

"Are you sure the kids are okay with that?"

"They will be. They like to travel, and it's not permanent. Just for the year."

She was silent for a while. "Well, at least let your father share some of his miles with you. Lord knows how many that man's racked up."

"We'll be fine, Mom. Honestly."

"Okay, well, check in occasionally. Let me know you're all still alive."

"I will."

"And be careful, okay?" Her voice was soft. Vulnerable in a way I'd never heard it.

"We will."

"Okay, I have to go. Matt's helping me to fix a broken fence post in the backyard."

"Matt the neighbor?"

"Don't say it like that, as if he's *just* the neighbor."

"He is *just* the neighbor, Mom. You *just* met him."

"I'll have you know that sometimes...two souls just connect."

"Did you just tell me you think he's your soul mate?" I grimaced.

"Oh, Ainsley, honestly. Don't be ridiculous. I'm going now. Goodbye."

With that, she ended the call and I shook my head, too worried about my own problems to concern myself with my mother's. Even if, for a split second, she'd managed to find her heart, I had years of experience to tell me it wouldn't last long. Whatever sort of sentimental itch my mother had gotten, I knew who she was down deep. Maybe she was just bored. Maybe she was feeling guilty over our fight. Either way, she'd find something else to busy herself with soon, and the kids and I would be just another thing she didn't have time for.

Maybe Matt would be the next project she took on. All I knew was that I was done concerning myself with other people's lives before my own.

I'd saved my children. They were safe with Glennon and Seth, I had no doubts.

Now, it was time to save myself.

CHAPTER TWENTY

PETER

Two hours after I'd been attacked and abandoned by my wife, I stood in the quiet hallway of my office. It was strange, really, how much of my life was spent within these walls. How much time and energy I put into making it something great. When Ainsley and I first dreamed of building Lae Haer, it seemed impossible. Without money or experience, who were we to try to build a company? But we tried and failed more than once.

We were on the brink of failure again, the company ready to go under, when I approached her about bringing in an investor. She'd been hesitant initially, but I'd pushed. It was my judgment, my vision, that saved my company. Beckman had been unsure too, originally; he'd actually told me no once or twice. He didn't know much about architecture, but he did know about business. That was what I needed. After a few meetings, I'd gotten him to come around.

Persistence. The unwillingness to take no for an answer. Those were my strengths.

I could be persuasive, I knew.

I always had been. Maisy had gotten it from me, Ainsley often said.

People could be talked into just about anything if you refused to accept the word "no." That was what it was going to take with my wife, I knew. I wouldn't give up. I'd never give up, and she knew it.

I rapped my knuckles against the wood of the office door next to mine, twisting the knob and leaning my head inside.

"Hey," Gina said, checking the time. "I didn't think you were in this week."

"I'm not. Not officially." I walked into the office and shut the door, taking a seat in front of her. "I need the corporate card. Do you still have it from the dinner last month?"

"Um, I think so." She pulled open the bottom drawer of her desk and removed a black leather purse from inside of it. I checked behind me as I heard laughter from the hallway. "Jason's birthday," she said, answering a question I hadn't asked. I averted my attention back to her. "They're all celebrating."

I rested my arm on the back of the chair next to me. "Shouldn't you be out there, then?"

She shook her head, finally retrieving her wallet from inside the purse and locating the bright-blue card. "Here you go." She held it out for me. "I'm staying far away from cake until the wedding."

"Wedding?" I eyed her finger, which was bare. "You're getting married?"

"Lincoln proposed." She fought back a smile, but it was pointless.

"Lincoln? What—the fondue guy?"

"Well, if you mean he owns a restaurant that sells fondue, then yes, that's correct."

"I didn't know you two were engaged."

"It just happened." She wagged the card, a reminder she was still waiting for me to take it, and I reached forward, sliding it from between her fingers slowly.

"Congratulations."

She nodded. "Is that all you needed? I'm getting ready for a conference call."

"Uh, yeah." I reached in my back pocket and pulled out my wallet, sliding the card inside. "So, what? No cake because you're trying to fit in a wedding dress or something?"

She blinked slowly, processing what I'd said. "What a stupid, misogynistic question."

"S-sorry?"

"Why would I buy a wedding dress that would require me to change something about myself? The dress should fit me, not the other way around."

"I wasn't trying to suggest—"

"Not that it's any of your business, but I'm cutting out cake because dairy causes me to break out. I'd like to have clear skin on my wedding day. For *me*. Not him."

"Right. Cool. Makes sense."

She tapped her fingers on the top of her desk, glancing toward the screen. "Okay, well, if that's all..."

I stood from the chair. "Right. Sorry." Reaching the door, I pulled it open and disappeared into the hall without another word.

A voice stopped me. "Peter?"

"Beckman, hey." I waved as he used a bony finger to smooth one of his wild gray brows.

"What are you doing here?" He kept his distance, looking as if he might want to dart away, the germaphobe that he was. "I thought you were out sick this week."

"I just had to pick up a few things," I said. "And don't worry. I'm not contagious or anything. It's family stuff."

He took a cautious step toward me, but not too close, and nodded. "Everything alright?"

"Yeah," I assured him, then changed my tone slightly. If I was going to keep missing work and relying on the team to cover my workload, I needed to lose the cheery facade. "It's just...Ainsley and I are getting a divorce."

The wrinkles around Beckman's eyes deepened with obvious concern. "Do you have a good lawyer?"

"Not yet. I'm in the process of getting everything worked out."

"I've got a card." He pulled out his wallet. "You're sure you're not sick?"

"Positive. Healthy as a horse."

He walked toward me, retrieving a business card from his wallet. When he reached me, he passed it over and I stared down at the bent edges and a scrawled note that read, **_Lunch @ 12_**. "Call John. He's handled both my divorces. Good guy. He'll make sure you're taken care of."

"Thanks." I tapped a finger on the card before shoving it in my pocket. "I should get going."

"Of course. Me too. I've got a one fifteen." He tapped his watch and turned to go into the conference room on our right. I should've been in that meeting. I should've been working to build the company I started from the ground up.

But I didn't care to.

Nothing mattered but bringing my family home.

I was giving up so much in order to deal with Ainsley's drama.

The sacrifices, it seemed, were endless, and she'd never be grateful for any of them.

CHAPTER TWENTY-ONE

AINSLEY

When Peter answered the phone, the noise in the background told me he was somewhere outside. Somewhere crowded. "Where are you?"

"I'm...at work. Why?"

Had he really gone to work after what we'd just gone through? Could he be that callous? "Can you meet me somewhere?"

"Uh, sure. Like where? And why?"

"Things got out of hand before. We really do need to talk. I overreacted, and I'm sorry. I was worried and nervous, and...I'm sorry, too, if I hurt you. I was scared you were going to hurt me, and—"

"Ainsley, you know I'd never want to hurt you."

"I know that," I told him, pausing as I worked to catch my breath and veered the car off at the next exit, heading for downtown. "Look, let's just meet somewhere public. We can grab coffee and talk. No weapons. No threats.

Just...talk. We used to be able to do that, right? I'd like to think we still can."

"That sounds great. How about the coffee shop on Eighth?"

"Perfect. I can be there in twenty minutes."

"I'll get us a table."

TWENTY MINUTES LATER, I parked in front of the local comedy club and crossed two streets on my way to the coffee shop. Inside, Peter was waiting for me at a table in the back. I approached the counter and ordered a mint green tea, taking my time as I poured a packet of sweetener into the paper cup. I avoided looking at my husband, though I could feel his eyes burning into me from behind. He blended into the scenery around us. Easily faded into the background. He was just an average guy in a coffee shop.

Was that how he'd gotten away with things for so long?

Was that why he'd never been caught? Why no one ever suspected he could be dangerous?

Why *I* never suspected he could be dangerous?

I thought back to what I'd learned months ago—that when we'd met, I was meant to be his next victim. I supposed I was lucky that it hadn't ended that way, but that didn't mean he hadn't taken anything from me. Half my life had been wasted on him. On whatever this was.

Once I could no longer justify standing there, slowly

stirring the sweetener into the tea, I turned and met his eyes, crossing the room and taking a seat in front of him.

"Hey."

He nodded. "Hey." His fingers laced around the coffee cup in front of him, then went back under the table. "Thanks, uh, thanks for suggesting this." He scratched his cheek, looking around.

"I wanted to be able to talk things through."

He folded his hands in front of him, his thumbs tapping nervously against his knuckles. "Okay, sure. What things?"

"Well, now that things have calmed down, I want you to know that..." I pinched my lips together, staring at the cup of tea. "You weren't wrong before. What you said about me not being able to...you know."

When I looked back up, his brows were an inch higher than before, his eyes wide. "I wasn't?"

"Come on, you know you weren't." I rolled my eyes.

"It's nice to get a confirmation."

"You're my husband, Peter. The father of my children. Of course I love you. How could I not? I should've... I was hurt by what happened. I was hurt about...her. And I was vulnerable in a way I've never been vulnerable with you. I was trying, actively trying, and it felt like you weren't."

"I know," he said, reaching for my hand. I didn't budge. After a moment, he withdrew the gesture. "Everything with Joanna was a mistake. I love you, Ainsley. I love you so much. And I took you for granted, I know that. You were willing to give me everything, to change for me, and I still couldn't see what I had right in front of me. I'm sorry for that. But don't you think we can still work it out? Is there even a chance we can fix this?"

"I don't think so, Peter," I told him, spinning the cup in place on the table with one hand. "I... I think I've done all I can do."

"You don't have to do anything. You're perfect. I'll do it all."

I held up a hand. "Just...stop. Please. We've been down this road too many times. The bottom line is that we're dangerous for each other. We both deserve better—"

He shook his head wildly. "That's not true—"

"I love you, Peter. I will always love you. I wish it hadn't come down to this. I wish there was any other way, but there isn't." To my surprise, tears stung my eyes. "We have to move on, both of us, and the only way to do that is to get through this. It's the hardest part, but we have to."

He looked down, keeping his eyes trained on his coffee. "I...don't want that."

"I know. I don't either. But it's what's best for everyone involved."

"The kids?" When he looked back up at me, his eyes glistened with tears.

"Especially the kids."

"I love them." The first tear fell, and he brushed it away.

"I know that. *They* know that."

"Then how can this be the right thing?"

"Sometimes...even people who love each other aren't

meant to be together. For various reasons. Personalities, timing... It just doesn't work between us. I'm tired of struggling. I'm tired of fighting."

He was silent for a moment. "There has to be another way."

"I don't think there is. I'm going to take care of them, Peter. You know I will. I'll make sure they have good lives, I promise you."

"And what? I just... I just *disappear*?" His voice was too loud. The couple sitting three tables down eyed us suspiciously, and Peter stood.

I stood up too, trying to get him to calm down. "I never said that. Maybe we can come up with a new sort of arrangement. Where the kids can see you a few times a month. We can come and visit."

"Come from where?"

"Sit down, please. This is just a conversation." I gestured toward the seat and, when he finally took it, I sat down as well.

"Come and visit from where, Ainsley?" He repeated, not looking at me. "Where are you planning to go?"

"Wherever we'll be living at the time. I haven't decided anything yet."

"But I get no say in this?" He covered his mouth with his palm, then let it fall away, his eyes unfocused. "Is that really what you want?"

"I'm trying to be civil here, Peter. Short of us coming home and pretending nothing's changed, what can I give you that you want? I won't try to take any money, or any part of Lae Haer—"

He met my eyes then, his voice too loud. "Was that even a question?"

I lowered my voice when he raised his. "What do you want? Tell me. What is your ideal outcome here?"

"I want you to come home."

"It's not an option. Aside from that."

He huffed out a breath of air from his nose. "I want to be able to see the kids whenever I want."

"Okay. How often? Weekly? Monthly?"

"*Daily*, Ainsley, Jesus. You think I'd be fine seeing our children *monthly*? Be reasonable." He leaned back in his chair, looking like a petulant child.

"I *thought* I was." I rubbed my fingers, trying to ease the tension in them. "We have to compromise. For their sake."

"And how exactly are you compromising?"

"I'm starting over, Peter. Alone. I'm going to have to build a new career in a city where I don't know anyone. I'm going to be the sole provider for the kids on a day-to-day basis. Don't you consider that a sacrifice?"

"No, I consider it selfish, frankly."

"Selfish?"

"Yes, selfish. Have you even asked the kids what they want?"

Somewhere deep inside my stomach, I felt a sharp tugging sensation—as if the floor had fallen out from under me—as I recalled the conversation with Dylan the night before. I was nearly certain Maisy would choose me, but Dylan was a wild card. After our fight, I was almost positive he'd choose to stay with Peter if he was given the option. And Riley would follow his lead.

The idea of Peter raising the boys alone was devastating. What would he turn them into?

No.

It wasn't an option.

"I'm being their parent right now. What they want is irrelevant compared to what's best for them."

His gaze hardened. "Meaning?"

"Meaning the kids stay with me. It's nonnegotiable."

"Unless I get a lawyer."

"Come on," I said with a scoff.

"Come on what?"

"You're not going to hire a lawyer, Peter. We're going to talk this out like adults."

"Too late. I already have." He reached in his pocket and pulled out a white business card with creased corners. He pointed to the handwritten note at the top. "We met for lunch at noon. He thinks I stand a chance at full custody."

I picked up the card with shaking hands, reading over it. "Full custody? You can't be serious."

"Oh, I am. Come home, or I'll fight you with everything I have for them." He leaned forward, lowering his voice. "And I'll win."

Had I misread the situation so badly? The idea of my husband taking the initiative to get an attorney involved when I was sure he was still rebelling against the idea that we were getting divorced in the first place was shocking.

"H-how did you pay for it?" I asked. There was no money in the accounts, certainly not enough to retain an attorney.

"Yeah, I noticed you drained the accounts." He tapped the corner of a bright-blue card I didn't recognize in his wallet. "Did you think I didn't have a plan in place in case something like this were to ever happen?"

Yes, that's exactly what I thought.

I didn't say that. Instead, I said, "Well, if that's how you want to go about this, then I guess I'll hire one, too."

"Guess so."

"This is only going to make things harder on the kids. You realize that, right?"

"So move home and let's call it all off. If you are really thinking about the kids, that's what you'll do."

In his eyes, I saw the challenge. I tapped my phone screen, checking the time. Nearly an hour had passed since I'd called him. Since our meeting started.

Had anything been accomplished in that time?

"That's not an option," I said finally.

"Well, call my lawyer, then," he said, pushing up from the table to stand once again.

"Where are you going?" I stood, too, hurrying after him as he crossed the crowded coffee shop and shoved the door open. "Peter, wait!" I called, trying to keep my voice down as we stepped out onto the busy sidewalk. I moved aside as a group of young women scurried past us, laughing loudly at a joke we hadn't heard. "Wait!" I shouted, grabbing his arm.

"Wait for what?" He spun around, tearing his arm

away from me. "What could you possibly want me to wait for? What could we possibly still have to talk about?"

"I—" I tried to think, tried to find something I could say that would make sense.

"Unless you don't want me to leave," he offered, the anger dissipating from his voice.

"We aren't done talking."

"Oh, I think we are." He turned away from me again.

"I don't want you to leave," I blurted out, grabbing his arm again.

When he turned to face me, the smug grin on his face was enough to make me sick. "I knew it."

"Don't make this a thing."

"Why don't you want me to leave, Ainsley? Because you love me?"

"I'm..." I couldn't lie. "It's hard to walk away."

"Then don't." He closed the space between us in an instant, gathering up my hands in his. "Don't do this. Please." He lifted our hands to his lips and kissed my fingers. "I love you. I love our family. We can fix this. *You* can fix this. You fix everything else. Please fix this."

I was silent for a moment, trying to think. It was all too much. The conflicting emotions, the panic, the fear. The anger. "Can...can we go for a drive?"

He pulled the keys from his pocket triumphantly and jutted his head toward our SUV across the street. "Sure. Of course."

I followed him to the vehicle with apprehension, still

not sure it was the best idea, but it was the only idea I had.

He opened my door for me, waiting until I was inside before shutting it. Once he was in his seat, he locked the doors. I swallowed, gripping the door with sweating palms.

Breathe.

Just breathe.

"Now then, where to?" He started the SUV with a smile plastered on his lips. Would I ever be able to feel normal with him again? He pulled out of the parking space and outstretched his hand, waiting for me to place mine in his waiting palm.

When I did, he rubbed his thumb across my knuckles slowly, reminding me of the many times he'd done that to keep me calm. During labor with the kids, during a scary movie, during a particularly stressful dinner with my parents.

Once, Peter had been loving.

And then I'd met the monster.

Foolishly, I'd believed I could save the loving part of him, despite the monster's powers, but now...now, I knew differently. The evil inside my husband was never just a part of him. It was all of him.

His love was meant to wield power over us all.

And I'd almost let him win.

CHAPTER TWENTY-TWO

PETER

We drove hand in hand as if nothing bad had ever happened between us. As if the past few days and weeks had been merely a nightmare. Maybe one day, we'd look back and think that's all it was.

A guy could dream, anyway.

"The kids will be so excited," I said after a long while of riding in silence.

"Mhm," she agreed halfheartedly.

"I know you're worried. I get it, I really do. But I promise you, you're going to be so impressed with how much I've changed. I told you once before that you fixed me, but maybe that didn't stick. Now, though, this time it really worked. You scared me straight, Ains. I'll never, never hurt you again."

She nodded, then looked over at me and spoke with a soft voice, "How can you be sure?"

"Because I thought I'd lost you," I said with an exasperated sigh. "I thought I'd lost the kids. There's not much I'm afraid of in this world, Ainsley, but that tops the list."

She was silent, but I was winning her over. I could see it in her eyes. I wanted to make her remember who we'd been. Why we were still worth fighting for.

I pulled over when I spied a gas station.

"What are you doing?"

"You'll see. Wait here." I stepped out of the SUV and shut the door, locking it behind me just in case. Inside, I found a bag of her favorite chocolate-covered peanuts, two burgers, and a bottle of red wine. At the counter, I paid for the items and made my way back outside, swinging the bag carelessly around my wrist. The pure joy I felt in that moment was unlike anything I'd ever experienced.

Everything was going to work out.

She watched me approach apprehensively, and when I opened the door, she was fanning herself with her hand. "You could've left the keys."

I didn't respond. We both knew why I couldn't do that.

"What was that about, anyway?" she asked.

I pulled the wine, food, and candy from the bag. "Remember our second date?"

She eyed the candy, then the wine, and pulled them both toward her slowly, lost in thought. "Our reservation was bumped at the last minute because of some big dinner party."

"Right. And you'd been in class all day..."

"That's right!" Her eyes lit up. "I was starving."

"You were *starving*," I repeated, my breathing slowing as I recalled the memory. "So, we left and drove to the first place we could find, which was a gas station."

She giggled. "All I wanted was a burger and you brought me out a salad."

"I thought you were going to walk home after that," I said with a laugh. "It wasn't my fault, though. I'd never seen a girl order anything but a salad on a date."

"Salads aren't meals," she said, pursing her lips and shaking her head.

"About that, we could agree. It was our first *actual* dinner together, and we had gas station burgers and cheap wine, with chocolate-covered peanuts for dessert. And...it was the best date of my life."

She softened, her eyes searching mine. "Mine too."

"You...you weren't like other girls, Ains. I realized that when we met." *When I couldn't hurt you.* I didn't say that part aloud, but the truth of it was there between us. "And that was when I knew."

"Knew what?"

"That you were the person who could save me from myself."

She looked down, playing with the plastic bag of candy thoughtfully. "We used to be great, didn't we?"

"We still are," I told her, running a finger against the back of her arm. "We still can be."

When she didn't say anything else, I reached for her cheek. She turned to look at me almost hesitantly, and I lowered my lips to hers. Kissing her was as easy as breathing. Easier, maybe. It was the only thing that made sense in the moments that made no sense at all. I was sure most of our problems could be solved if she'd just let our kiss take her back to who we used to be. If she would just let our kiss remind her of those people.

As quickly as it started, it ended. She turned away, staring out the window, and whispered, "Thank you, Peter. This was really kind of you."

Taking it in stride, I touched her wrist gently, sliding my hand into her palm. "Of course."

"Where are we going?" she asked, as I started the vehicle and drove out of the lot.

"Home," I told her, gripping the wheel. "So we can talk more."

Or not talk at all. That would be my preference.

She pulled out her phone, checking it.

"Do you have somewhere to be?"

"No. I was just checking the time," she said. "My car is still parked on the street. I didn't plan to leave it for long."

"We'll come back for it."

She nodded, not protesting, and turned up the radio.

"Aren't you going to eat?" I asked, pointing at the untouched food in her lap.

"Maybe once we get there. I'm not too hungry." She wasn't looking at me, but I tried not to take it to heart. I knew things were going to be strange between us for a while. I could handle strange, as long as she was with me.

Half an hour later, when we pulled into our long driveway, something shifted in Ainsley. She sat up straighter in the seat, checking her phone again, and I noticed how white her knuckles were as she gripped the door handle.

She was nervous. Scared, maybe. But she had nothing to worry about.

"Everything okay?"

"You were right, Peter," she said again, repeating what she'd told me at the coffee shop.

"Hm?"

"I can't kill you. I'm so sorry."

"Well, I think I'll manage to forgive you," I said with a chuckle under my breath, trying to piece together what she was saying and why she suddenly looked so worried.

"I can't kill you," she repeated for the third time, "but that doesn't mean I can't protect myself and my children from you."

As she said the words, we rounded the corner and the truth smacked me in the chest. The driveway was lined with police cars and various official vehicles. My blood ran ice cold.

No.

"What did you do, Ainsley?"

"The only thing I *could* do," she whispered. When she met my eyes, there were tears in hers.

I swallowed, considering backing up and driving away just as I saw a police cruiser pulling into the driveway behind me. It was a setup. She'd planned all of this. I was trapped. This was over.

I swallowed, looking at her warily. "I'd rather you'd have killed me."

CHAPTER TWENTY-THREE

AINSLEY

"Ainsley, what did you do?" he asked again, shaking his head in disbelief. "You can't be serious."

"You gave me no choice. I had to do it for the kids."

I spied Detective Burks making her way toward us, not looking particularly pleased.

"Who is that?" Peter asked.

"The detective working our case," I said, reaching for my door and stepping out of the car, meeting her halfway. I felt as if I were going to be sick.

"Mrs. Greenburg." She said my name as a full sentence, and I couldn't read her emotions.

My hands were freezing, and I clutched them together in front of my stomach. "Detective. I'm sorry to have to do this—"

"What's this all about?" Peter asked. I heard the car door shut and the crunch of the gravel underneath his shoes before he appeared next to me.

"Oh, just doing a bit of light gardening," she said. "You a big gardener, Mr. Greenburg?"

"Can't say that I am." The skin of his neck flushed pink.

"Really? Well, your wife says differently." She eyed me, and soon enough, they were both looking at me.

"What's she talking about, Ainsley?"

"I told her about the bodies, Peter. About the email you were planning to send, the one I found—your confession. I told her about the women. I gave them permission to excavate the woods. To give their families peace. I'm so sorry."

He stared at me with a blank look in his eyes, as if I were speaking a language he couldn't understand. "I'm sorry, what are you talking about? Is this a joke?" He pointed a finger gun at the detective. "Is this a prank? Did Beckman put you up to this?" He looked around as if waiting for someone to jump out of the woods and shout, 'Surprise!'

"I'm afraid this is no joke, Mr. Greenburg." The detective studied him silently for a few moments.

Peter looked at me, his expression turning stony. "Is this because of the divorce? Is this your way of getting back at me?"

"Divorce?" the detective asked, folding her arms across her chest as she stared at me.

"My wife and I are in the process of getting a divorce," Peter told her. "It's been very messy and painful for the two of us. I'm really sorry if she brought you here and wasted your time, but surely you have to realize she's joking. I mean, do I look like a killer to you?"

"You do know most serial killers are middle-aged white men, don't you?" she snapped.

"Right." Peter looked down. "Well...I mean, there are no bodies here, so whatever she's told you, she's wrong. And this is my property, too. Don't you need my permission as well as hers?"

"As luck would have it, no. I don't."

I suppressed a smile.

"Your wife forwarded me an email with a confession, allegedly from you, claiming you've killed multiple people and buried their bodies in your woods. The email contained the exact location of the bodies, including longitude and latitude, and a marked-up Google map. Care to explain?"

"I don't know anything about any email," he said firmly, waving his hands to the side as if he were an umpire calling someone *safe*. "This has gone far enough. Ainsley, seriously, you've done a lot of terrible shit, but is this really how you want this to be? I thought we could be civil. But filing a fake police report?"

"It's not fake, and you know it!" I argued. Why weren't they arresting him already? Why wasn't the detective backing me up?

"There are no bodies in the woods," he said, his fingers near his temples.

I shot a glance at Detective Burks as she held up a hand to stop the argument.

"As it turns out, Mrs. Greenburg, he's right."

"What?" The swooping sensation in my core was back. The ground all but torn out from underneath me. "What do you mean?"

She gestured toward the crowd of detectives and officers milling about around the perimeter of the house. Looking closer, I realized they were all making their way back toward their cruisers. "We excavated the marked area, and the entire surrounding area on your word that there was something to find and there wasn't. No bodies. Just what looked like the skeleton of an old dog."

"Scout..." I whispered. "That's not possible. Are you sure you checked the right spot?"

"As I said, we checked the exact area that was marked on the map—it didn't leave a whole lot of guesswork—and all of the surrounding area."

"What did you do?" I demanded, turning to Peter as my throat constricted with rage.

He ignored me completely. "I'm so sorry, Detective. Honestly. I'm embarrassed."

The detective stared at him. "We also checked the room where your wife claims you've held women hostage."

His brows knitted together with an almost amused scoff. "The *what?*"

"In the garage." She was no longer talking to me. Only to Peter. I was the irrational woman trying to get revenge on her husband for leaving her.

"The *safe* room?" he asked, looking unimpressed. "Seriously, Ainsley?" He crossed his arms. "I'm going to guess you didn't find anything in there except dust and old tools, right?"

The detective didn't immediately confirm it.

"I'm a bit of an over preparer. Without a basement, I just felt safer having a room we could go to in case of a tornado. It comes in handy. But..." He laughed, as if it was ridiculous he even had to say it. "I can assure you the only people being tortured in there are my kids when they have to listen to my jokes during a tornado warning. Have you heard the one about a tornado's favorite game?" His eyes twinkled, as if he had no cares in the world. "Twister. Get it?" He broke out in laughter over the terrible joke. I felt like I was watching the entire thing playing out in slow motion. This wasn't how this was supposed to go.

When the detective didn't laugh along, he straightened up, clearing his throat. "My kids don't think it's funny either. That was probably the worst of them. I've got more—"

"That's really not necessary, Mr. Greenburg." She met my eyes again. "We didn't find anything in the room either. There's nothing here to suggest any of what you said or anything from that email is true. No black bag in the space in the wall, no traces of blood, no bodies in the woods."

"It's not possible," I said, finding my voice again as I watched my chance to finally end this slipping away. I'd been so close. "I don't know how he did it, Detective, but I promise you, he had to have moved the bodies. They're there. They have to be."

"And you know this how, Mrs. Greenburg? Because he wrote some email? There's no proof that your husband wrote that email at all, other than it being sent from his email address, which you, no doubt, have access to. I'm not here to play marriage counselor. The taxpayers are not paying for us to come out here and ruin each other's days for you guys. Filing a fake police report is a very serious matter. I could have you arrested—"

"It wasn't false. I swear to you, it wasn't. This is what he does. He had to have known I was going to turn him in. He knew I found the email. He knew I'd tell you where the bodies were."

"Do you have any proof that the bodies existed at all? Anything besides the email?"

"No, nothing, but—"

"Had you ever seen them with your own eyes?"

Peter was staring at me now, too. Obviously enjoying this all a bit too much.

"No."

"Then our work here is done." She held her hand up with what must've been a signal, because the remaining officers began retreating to their cars, their work obviously done.

"Wait, *wait!*" I shouted as one final idea occurred to me. "Please...check under the patio. There's a body under the patio."

Detective Burks glanced over at the concrete patio, then back at Peter. Finally, she looked at me. "The letter didn't mention that. I thought you said all the bodies were in the woods."

It was my only chance. This was the only shot I had. There was no way Peter had moved Stefan's or Illiana's bodies, which meant they could still be found.

"They were. They...are. They should be. But there was one. He told me about it when I found the email. It's why he put the patio down last summer."

The detective blew a piece of hair from her eyes. "Look, Mrs. Greenburg, I don't know what's going on, but it seems an awful lot like you're trying to play with me. I'm not going to waste any more time, energy, or resources on digging up your patio when we just had to dig up your woods."

"Oh, please, no. If you'll just dig it up, I promise you, you'll see that—"

"If you can find me proof—" She held up her hand to cut me off. "I will listen. But otherwise, I advise the two of you to separate—at least for the night, but preferably for a long, *long* time—and cool off."

"Thank you, Detective. We will," Peter said, bowing to her as if he were practicing martial arts. I felt as if I were living in some alternate universe. How was any of this happening?

"Detective, please, if you'll just listen—"

"I *have* listened, Mrs. Greenburg. I'm done listening now. I'm sorry." She took another step back, but hesitated. "One last question." She was looking at Peter. "If you're not a gardener..." I felt bitter hope fill my chest. "Why has so much of your property been disturbed in the last few months?"

"Ex-excuse me?"

She turned back to face us. "Well, it's obvious quite a bit of the area Mrs. Greenburg directed us to had recently been disturbed. Now, if you were a gardener, I guess that might make sense. But since you've already said you're not..." She paused. "Would you care to explain?"

He shot a glance at me, then straightened his shoulders. "I...I'm not exactly sure where you were looking, but I'm in the early stages of clearing out some of the woods to build an extra workspace for my architecture firm. I'm hoping it'll mean I can be home with the kids more— work from home and all that. Especially once we divide up custody. I've been digging around, preparing to lay the foundation and, like you saw, we have buried quite a few family pets out there and there are coyotes in the woods. I couldn't say for sure which one caused what you saw. I'm happy to answer more questions if you want to show me the exact area."

She was silent for a moment, then her lips pressed into a thin smile with a puff of breath from her nose. Her chest fell with the heavy release of air. "That won't be necessary. I've taken up enough of your time." Somehow, I thought she wanted to say we'd taken up enough of hers. She opened her mouth, obviously weighing what she was about to say. "Mr. Greenburg, I should ask if you want to press charges against your wife for the false allegations."

He beamed at her, mocking sincerity. "Oh, no, it's okay. Thank you, Detective. We don't want to waste any more of *your* time. Tensions are just high right now. I'm really sorry you had to come all the way out here for this."

She looked at me one last time, then turned on her heel and made her way to her car. The officers pulled down the driveway slowly, one by one, none of them bothering to look at us. Peter waved at them like a politician, a giant grin on his face.

"What did you do?" I asked him through gritted teeth. I didn't care who saw how angry I was. It was impossible. It was also my last idea. I had no idea what I was going to do now.

Once the cars were gone, all except the two unmarked cars driven by Detective Burks and another detective, an excavator was driven down the side of our yard and around the curve of our driveway. Finally, the detectives pulled away, leaving us standing in silence, the weight of what just happened hanging in the air between us.

I'd failed.

I'd failed miserably.

"What did you do, Peter?" I demanded again.

"Looks like I just saved my own ass, doesn't it?" He chuckled. "Did you honestly think I'd leave them where they were, knowing you tried to kill me? I love you, Ains. But I'm not stupid enough to trust you. Not anymore. You ruined that."

"Where are the bodies?"

"Looks like I'm the only one who knows." He shrugged, walking toward the end of the driveway. I followed him. "And if you'd like to keep it that way, I suggest you do as I say."

"Where are you going?"

He rounded the corner, peering down the portion of the driveway that was concealed from the house. "Checking to make sure they left. Wouldn't want to walk into another trap." When he turned back to me, he cracked his knuckles. "Now then, where were we?"

Thinking quickly, I spun around on my heels, tearing down the driveway at breakneck speed. He rushed to keep up, lunging at me with his hands outstretched. He grabbed my arm, and I jerked forward. I tried to swipe the keys from his hand, but he held on to them tightly, tugging me into his chest and wrapping me up with both arms.

Using all my strength, I pulled his wrist to my lips, sinking my teeth into his skin with so much force, I tasted blood in seconds. I bit down harder until I felt a chunk of skin break free. He jerked back, cursing at me and dropping the keys. Fighting against the urge to vomit, I spit the piece of skin onto the ground and dove for the keys.

I scooped them up and scrambled to my feet, sliding inside while he cursed and kicked and spun in circles with pain. When the car started, he was jarred from his pain-filled trance. He hurried forward, but he was too slow.

I stomped on the gas and the car flew down the driveway in reverse, narrowly making the turn. I silently prayed that the police would still be there. That they'd see him chasing me, but I knew they'd be gone. They weren't wasting time with us, and I couldn't blame them.

This made twice now that Peter had bested me, but it wouldn't happen again. He was getting smarter, I'd give him that, but I'd always been—and would always be—able to outsmart him. I'd just have to learn to play by the new rules of the game.

CHAPTER TWENTY-FOUR

PETER

Ainsley had tried to turn me in.

First, she'd tried to kill me. Then, when that hadn't worked, she'd tried to turn me in. She wanted me to go to prison. To pay for what I'd done—what *we'd* done, someone should remind her. If I hadn't had the foresight to move the bodies—what was left of them, anyway—I might never see my children again.

Ainsley had believed she'd won.

It sickened me...realizing that was why she wanted to meet me. She was keeping me occupied. Keeping me out of the way. Then, she let me drive us straight into the trap without a single care. How could anyone be so heartless? So cruel?

Luckily for me, once again, I'd outsmarted her.

I was getting good at that.

Now though, I was home without a car and a chunk of skin missing from my wrist. I doused it in cool water, patting it with a gauze pad.

What an animal she was...

Before I wrapped the wound, I picked up my phone to snap pictures. If she was going to try to take me down, I would do the same. No judge could see pictures of this abuse and think she could be a fit parent.

I didn't want it to come to that, but if it had to, it was better to be safe than sorry. Ainsley had already proven she'd stop at nothing to win. I'm not sure why I expected anything different.

I positioned the phone's camera over my wrist and took two pictures, one from farther away and one up close. You could make out the teeth marks plainly, and the way the skin around the wound had already begun to bruise.

My phone buzzed, interrupting my thoughts, and I looked down.

Well, well, well...

I didn't really have time to answer, but I couldn't resist. After all, why would Gina be calling me? Ever since our unfortunate encounter with Mallory during my arrangement with Ainsley, things had been awkward between us at best and cool at worst. Today's conversation in the office hadn't exactly left me expecting to hear from her again.

"Hello?" I kept my voice calm, cool, and casual.

"Hey, is this a bad time?"

"No. Not at all." I braced the phone between my shoulder and ear as I carefully wrapped my wrist, wincing from the pain. "What's up?"

"It's none of my business, but I couldn't help overhearing your conversation with Beckman today. About the divorce."

"Oh, right, yeah." I tore a piece of medical tape with my teeth and used it to press the final piece of gauze down.

"I'm sorry if I was rude to you today. I had no idea you were going through so much."

Suddenly able to focus my entire attention on the conversation, I sighed. "Oh, well, thanks. I'm...you know, I'm okay. It's been a long time coming. Ainsley and I... we're just in different places."

"I get it. I know things have been weird between us..." She didn't bother to elaborate when things had shifted. We both knew. "But if you ever need anything, I'm here. I truly wished things would get better for you guys."

"Thanks, Gina." Suddenly, I had the answer to my problems. Or...at least my biggest one at the moment. I needed a car. "You know, the hardest part is that she's taken my kids away from me."

"What do you mean?"

"She took them. Moved them out while I was at work. And now..." I paused for dramatic effect, allowing my voice to crack slightly. Still a manly cry, but a cry nonetheless. "Now, I have no idea where they are. She even stole my SUV today when she came over to talk. I...I shouldn't be saying this. I don't want to speak badly about her, but...I'm worried she's going to do something to hurt them. Or herself. Or me." I let the words hang in the air between us, before adding. "But I'll be okay. Somehow."

"Peter, if you really believe your wife is dangerous, you should call the police."

"Oh, I did. But there's no proof. You know they always side with the mother on these sorts of things."

"Well, I'm really sorry it's come to that. Is there...is there anything I can do?"

"Actually, there is." I gathered the medical supplies and shoved them back into the first aid kit, not bothering to put anything back in its place. Ainsley would hate it. "Could you give me a ride somewhere?"

"Oh, I don't know, Peter... I really don't want to get involved. I just wanted to apologize because it's been bothering me—"

"It's nothing crazy. I just need to get our car from downtown. I had Ainsley meet me for coffee and we rode back here together, but, like I said, she took my SUV. Her car is downtown, so I just need to pick it up."

"I'm not going to, like, get arrested for helping you steal her car, am I?"

I laughed. "No. Of course not."

"Okay, fine. Where should I pick you up?"

I rattled off the address.

"GPS shows I can be there in an hour."

"Okay, I'll be here. And thanks, Gina. This means a lot."

"I told you to get your shit together, Peter. Sounds like you finally are."

. . .

JUST UNDER AN HOUR LATER, Gina's gray Camry pulled into the driveway. I jogged out to the car to meet her, waving my injured hand at her in the fading daylight. When I opened the door, she leaned over, trying to get a better look at me.

"What happened to your hand?"

"Ainsley."

"She hurt you?"

"I'm fine."

"Peter, if she hurt you, you have to call the police. Men can be victims, too. There's no shame in—"

"I'm fine, Gina," I said gently. "I promise I'm fine. It's complicated with my kids. And I appreciate what you're saying, but tensions are already high. I just want to protect them."

"How are you going to do that?"

I gave a dry laugh, looking down at my hand hopelessly. "I have no idea."

"Have you talked to anyone else about this? If not the police, maybe a therapist? A friend?"

I looked up at her, knowing I was winning her over by the way she was staring at me. This was a new side to our relationship. One I didn't know existed before. "I'm talking to you."

She swallowed, her eyes darting back and forth between mine, and then looked away. She gripped the steering wheel. "I want to help you."

"You *are* helping me."

"I mean...I want to help you find your kids."

"No," I said quickly. "No. I can't ask you to get involved."

"You're not asking. I've seen the way you talk about your kids. I've seen the pictures on your desk. I've been with you on business trips when you stop to pick something up for them from the gift shop or when you order their favorite desserts from a restaurant to bring home after a work dinner. I don't know anything about your marriage, Peter, and I won't pretend to. And I know we aren't exactly friends. But if I'm all you've got, I want to help you. However I can."

"Why?" I couldn't make sense of it.

"Because, despite all evidence to the contrary"—she chuckled—"you're a pretty good guy. And you don't deserve this." She gestured toward my hand. "So let me help."

I nodded slowly, contemplating. "Okay."

"Okay?"

"If you're sure."

"I'm not," she admitted. "But it feels like the right thing to do, and I need a clean conscience walking into my marriage."

"Thank you, Gina," I said, buckling in as she pulled out of the driveway.

"So, where to?"

CHAPTER TWENTY-FIVE

AINSLEY

I'd finally worked up the courage to color my hair with the box dye I bought at the store. It felt strange —like staring into the face of a stranger. I only had nail scissors in my purse, but I knew I had to cut the length, too, so I worked slowly and diligently, chopping off strand by strand until my hair was chin length all the way around.

It was a terrible job—the cut was uneven and the color made me look washed out and lifeless—but it would have to do until I could get into a salon. My phone chimed, and I dashed across the room, opening up my email and staring at it in disbelief.

The subject line alone was enough to take my breath away: **Request Denied.**

Picking up the phone with trembling hands, I dialed my boss's number.

I was convinced she wouldn't answer by the fifth

ring, but just as I was prepared to hang up and call the office line, she did.

"Hello?"

"Tina, it's Ainsley. I just received your email about my request to transfer…"

"Mhm. Look, I'm sorry, Ainsley. As much as I'd hate to lose you, even if I wanted to transfer you, I couldn't. It's not up to me. It would have to go through HR, and they say we need you here."

"Who says? Jenn? She just approved Sara's transfer when she moved to New Orleans last year. How is this any different?"

"Listen, you're lucky they didn't fire you because you still haven't turned in your forms for leave. I had to fight for that."

"What? I…could've sworn I turned them in." I thought back, trying to recall the moment Tina had mentioned them. Had I been interrupted by Tara before or after that? Did I truly forget to send in the forms? How could I be so stupid? "I'm so sorry, Tina. I don't know how I managed to forget. I'll get them turned in today. Will they reconsider then?"

"I'm sorry, Ainsley, but no, I don't think so. Tara's leaving, your branch is barely hanging on by a thread, you still haven't even looked at the candidates I've sent you to fill her position. I know you're going through some things, but the bottom line is there was no way I was going to get them to approve a transfer on top of everything else going on. Denver's a new market. They want the best of… They want managers with proven track records."

"This is the first time I've had any issues. You know that. You know me. I've done everything for this company."

"I'm not arguing any of that, but *again*, it's not up to me."

"Then who is it up to? Who do I need to talk to?"

"Burt Stover."

"*Who?*" I pinched the skin on the inside of my wrist, the pain keeping me focused.

"The new head of HR. He doesn't know you like Jenn did. If she was still here, maybe she'd reconsider, but it's just rotten timing. I wish there was more I could do."

"Tina, please, I need this transfer. I have to have a job when I get out there. It doesn't even have to be Colorado. Do they need me somewhere else? Somewhere outside of Nashville? I'm not picky. I just can't stay here. But I have kids—two of which are accident-prone teenagers—and my husband's company is small. We rely on me to provide our health insurance."

She sighed. "Look, I'm not going to sugarcoat this. They're not pleased with the fact that you've missed two weeks' worth of work, are trying to move suddenly and rather urgently, and have just drained your accounts after having them with us for years. One of those things is bad enough, but put them together... Ainsley, I need you to be honest with me here. I can't help you if I don't know what's going on. Are you in some sort of trouble?"

"No," I assured her too quickly. "It's nothing like that." Then, because I felt like I needed some sort of excuse, I added, "My kids are having trouble at school.

164

My daughter specifically." Tina's daughter was around Maisy's age. If there was anything she'd sympathize with, this was it. "She's being bullied, and I'm not going to allow it to continue. The school isn't doing anything about it, and I'm done. I have to get her out of there. But I don't want to leave this company. I would think my loyalty would mean something here."

"Even if that's the case, and I can certainly understand it if it is, why would you take the money from your accounts? You know how that looks."

I tried to think quickly, to piece together any sort of excuse that would make sense. "Because one of the parents we're having issues with also works for this company. I'm not saying he would do anything, but I just thought it was better to protect ourselves in case things get ugly."

"What do you mean? Is this something I need to get HR involved in? Do you have reason to believe he's been looking at your accounts?"

"No. I don't even know that he realized I work here, but I recognized his name in a meeting we had with the school. It was a precaution. You know me, always prepared."

She was typing something when she spoke again. "Okay, I'll talk to Burt about the transfer, see if I can get him to reconsider, but no promises. Just...just get the form put in for your leave."

"I will. Thank you, Tina."

"Don't thank me yet. Talk soon."

I ended the call, my fingers still shaking. I'd never

considered the fact that I might lose my job or that my transfer request might get denied. Ever since I'd made the decision to leave, I'd been counting on the assurance that I'd still have a job. A stable job with insurance in order to take care of my children.

If I didn't, who was to say Peter might not win sole custody? If he already had a lawyer, he was a step ahead of me anyway.

When my phone buzzed again, I assumed it would be Tina with an update, but my hope was dashed when I saw my mother's name.

"Hello?"

"Hi, it's me."

"Everything okay?"

"Hm? Oh, yes, everything's fine. Fine. I'm just out running errands, and I picked up a few things for you and the kids. Do you care if I drop them by? Some snacks, and a few games and books to keep them occupied in the hotel and on the flight."

She must've been feeling much guiltier than I realized, because Mom was never the type to just pick something up while she was out. Either that or maybe she'd just realized how distressed I was. Perhaps even terrible mothers had mother's intuition.

"Oh, you didn't have to do that."

"Well, if it's the last time I'll be seeing you for a while, I wanted to. Do you want to come by the house later? Or would you rather I bring them to you?"

"Um...I'm not sure."

"Well, let me drop them off, then. I'm already out. Where are you staying?"

"I, um..." I looked down. "I'll just come get them at some point this afternoon."

"Why won't you tell me where you are? Is something wrong?"

"It's not that, it's just... Things got really heated between Peter and I. *And I know what you're going to say, so please just save it.* I don't want him to know where we are."

"What happened?"

"It was nothing." I didn't mention that I'd spent the night scrubbing his blood from my teeth. "Just a fight. But right now, I'm worried if he finds the kids, he'll try to take them away from me—"

"Oh, I'm sure he wouldn't do that."

"I'm sure there are parts of your marriage with Dad that I don't know about, just like there are parts of mine you don't know. Peter can't find out where I'm staying, and I don't want him to see me out and try to follow me—"

"Okay, fine, but what does any of that have to do with me?"

"I'm afraid he'll follow you too, Mom. He came to your house, so obviously he thinks we might be in touch. If he believes you know where I am, if he thinks there's any chance you could lead him to me, to us, I'm afraid he'll follow you."

She laughed. "Don't be ridiculous, Ainsley. Peter's not going to follow me. This isn't a spy mission."

"I need you to not come to me right now, Mom. Do you understand? I need you to just trust me. Hear me. Hear what I am saying and respect it."

"Fine, fine... But I want to get these to you somehow. Should we plan a drop? Maybe we could dress all in black and I'll sit down on a bench with a briefcase. We could come up with a code word—"

"*Mom!*" I cried, my irritation growing. "Just stop. Please stop making me feel stupid for protecting myself. I appreciate the gesture, but honestly, it's not necessary. I told you we had everything."

"You're taking my grandchildren away without even letting me say goodbye to them. The least you can do is let me give them a gift."

"It's not safe," I warned, my voice a low whisper. Why wasn't she understanding? Why didn't she believe me?

"Okay, well, let me have it delivered, then. How could he possibly know to follow a delivery man?"

Releasing an exasperated sigh, I thought it over. "Fine." I didn't have the strength to keep finding reasons to say no. "Okay, sure. That should work."

"Lovely. I'm ready when you are."

I told her the name of the hotel and the room number, and was relieved when she didn't criticize the place.

"Excellent." She clicked her pen. "I'll drop it off to be delivered in the next hour, so keep an eye out. You'll be there, right?"

"We'll be here. And thanks, Mom." It felt awkward to say.

"You're welcome. Be sure to tell them it's from me, not your father."

"I will."

TWO HOURS LATER, someone knocked on the door of the hotel. I held the stun gun in one hand as I approached it with soft steps. I pressed my face to the door, staring out the peephole.

The familiar face waiting for me took a moment to register.

"Matt?" I swung the door open, heat already warming my cheeks. I ran a hand over my hair, smoothing it down. "What on earth are you doing here?"

Upon seeing me, he did a double take. "Hey, I— Whoa, you look...your hair...it's...different." His gaze narrowed, scrutinizing me, then he overcorrected quickly. "*Good* different. I mean, not that you didn't look good before, you did..." He took a deep breath, then shook his head. "Sorry. Let me start over." He held out the plastic bags in his hands. "Your mom didn't tell you I was coming?"

"Uh, no, she...she said she was having something delivered, but..."

"Well, apparently I'm the delivery boy." He laughed, running a hand through the curly brown hair atop his head. "You, uh, hurt or sick or something?" He eyed the room over my shoulder. "I thought you lived around here. Why are you staying in a hotel?"

I stepped farther over so he couldn't see inside the room. Though it wasn't as disastrous as it would've been if the kids were still there, it certainly wasn't ready for company.

"Oh, I'm just hiding out for a few days. Escaping life. You know, the usual." The honesty in my words didn't register on his face.

He grinned, as if I'd made a joke. "Awesome. Cool. Um, how's that tire holding up?"

"Great. Thank you so much again. I really appreciate it."

"Oh, anytime. I was glad to help."

I smiled, then looked down, peering into the bag. As I'd suspected, my mother had gotten everything wrong. A romance book for Maisy that she'd have no interest in. Coloring books for...who knew, honestly.

"Well, yeah, there you go." He broke my concentration, gesturing toward the bags.

"Thanks. You really didn't have to do this."

"Oh, no. It was...it was..." When he looked at me again, there was that same sense of heightened curiosity I'd only ever seen coming from him. His eyes lit up as he stared at me. "It was really nice to see you again."

"You too." I grinned with one corner of my mouth.

He nodded slowly, opening his mouth as if he were going to say something before closing it again. He waved a fist in the air, then turned to walk away, but stopped. When he spoke, his words came out rushed. "Hey, listen,

I'm not very good at this sort of thing, but...how long are you going to be *hiding out?*"

Something fluttered in my chest. "Oh, I don't know exactly. A few more days, I think."

"Would I be totally off base if I asked if you wanted some company? I mean, dinner or something. Drinks, too. Drinks would be cool. Like...like a date?" He appeared swollen with hope—his chest puffed, upper lip sweating. I hesitated, and he jumped in with a chuckle. "Feel free to let me down easy if that was weird."

"It wasn't weird," I assured him, my insides doing cartwheels. I'd never felt so stupidly light-headed. I clamped my hands together, determined to shut this down quickly. "I'm just kind of in a not-so-good place right now. I don't think it's a good idea. I'm sorry. Trust me, it's not you."

"No, I get it." He bobbed his head slowly. "I didn't think I stood a chance anyway, but you know, I'd kick myself if I didn't try." He gripped the back of his neck with a boyish grin.

"Can I ask how old you are?" I asked him, curiosity getting the best of me.

He looked down with a hint of scarlet on his tanned cheeks. "I'm twenty-five." *Jesus Christ.* When he looked back up, his sage-green eyes drilled into mine. "Is that a bad thing?"

I broke eye contact in an attempt to clear my head. What the hell was wrong with me? I was being absurd. "You're...very young."

"Age is just a number." He shrugged. "Does that scare you?"

"A little," I admitted. "I'm...I'm nearly double your age. Doesn't *that* scare *you*? Shouldn't you be more interested in someone your own age?"

"Maybe. Probably, in fact. But..." He rested a hand on the wood of the doorframe. "I can't stop thinking about you. Ever since I met you. That has to mean something, doesn't it?"

It was my turn to break eye contact, my own cheeks flaming with heat. "I... Look, Matt, I'd be lying if I said you weren't attractive. But my life is complicated." I rolled my eyes. "So complicated. I'm just not really in a place to date right now. I'm sorry."

"No, I get it. I do."

"But I'm flattered," I offered. "Truly flattered. And in another life...who knows?"

He patted the doorframe. "Another life."

I smiled at him halfheartedly, fighting down any desire I might have to invite him inside. It was ridiculous. Stupid. Ridiculously stupid. Not to mention dangerous. Matt deserved so much better than whatever I could offer him right now, hiding in a hotel room, trying to conceal my identity while on the run from my murderous husband.

"Well," he said, after a beat, "I'll see you around then, Ainsley. And...if you change your mind, the offer stands."

I smiled at him softly before he turned to walk away. Once he was gone, I shut the door, my heart thundering in my chest. If I was Peter, I'd have taken him up on the offer. That was the difference between him and me. I could resist temptation, control my urges. That was why I was the better parent. I'd never put anyone or anything, myself included, before my children.

Peter could've never said the same.

CHAPTER TWENTY-SIX

PETER

Ainsley's car smelled of her. It was the first thing I noticed upon getting it back. It made being without my wife even more painful than it already was. Of course, as I rode alongside Gina the next day, I didn't bring it up. She didn't need to know how pathetic I was, though looking pathetic had apparently been enough to get me back in her good graces.

"Do you really think she might be staying here?" Gina asked, when we pulled onto the street in front of Adele's house. I'd been avoiding parking in the street since getting accosted by the shirtless man, but most of the people in the neighborhood seemed to be at work during the day, and I was in a different car this time anyway, so I hoped that would be enough to keep me from getting berated by the neighbors for a few hours.

"Probably not," I said. "Ainsley isn't stupid, and she knows I'm looking for her. But it's the only thing I have to go on. I'm hoping, if nothing else, Adele might lead me to her."

In truth, I couldn't believe Gina had agreed to this. Stalking my wife. Then again, I was sure she was just using it as an excuse to spend time with me again. We'd never gotten the chance before, and she'd practically begged for it at the time.

Once, I'd have given anything for extra time with Gina. Now, I'd take the company, but amusement was as far as my interests went. My loyalties still lay with Ainsley.

"Looks like someone's coming. Who is that?" she asked, pointing to the white pickup truck pulling into Adele's driveway.

"No idea." He stepped out of the truck, shielding his eyes from the sun as he looked over at us.

Gina sank down in her seat, pulling me down with her. She giggled. "Do you think he saw us?"

"I don't think so. He doesn't know who we are, even if he did."

I eased myself up in the seat, watching as the man headed for the front door. He knocked and, minutes later, my mother-in-law appeared in the doorway and allowed him inside.

"This is kind of fun," Gina said after a moment, breaking my concentration. "Like we're cops on a stakeout."

"It is, isn't it?" I agreed.

"You know, I was doing some research last night, and it seems like if you talk to your lawyer about filing for custody, even if it's just joint custody, they could help you locate your kids. It might be the best option."

I nodded, looking over at her. "I'm already talking with my lawyer about it, but without an address to find Ainsley, it's hard to serve her with papers."

"Do you think she'd go so far as to take them out of the country?"

I stared at her, not wanting to contemplate the possibility. It was enough to make me sick. "I don't want to believe it, no. But..." I gestured toward my wrist so she caught sight of the bandage again. "I guess you never really know someone, you know?"

"I'm worried about you, Peter."

"You don't need to worry about me. I appreciate your help with this, but I'm going to be fine. I have to believe that."

She was silent.

"Anyway, what does your fiancé think about you hanging out with me so much?"

"Why would he think anything about it?"

"Well, given our history, I just wondered if he was okay with this..."

"We went on one date that was interrupted," she said flatly, looking out the window. "I'd hardly call that history."

I gripped the steering wheel. "You're right. I never paid you back for that meal, either."

"I told you to keep it." She adjusted in her seat, turning to face me.

I grinned. "Well, you never lost your hair, so I guess Mallory wasn't too upset after all."

She gave a sly grin. "Not at me, anyway. Though she certainly had a lot of unflattering things to say about *you*." Her gaze raked down my body, and I shifted in place.

I chose my words carefully. "Well, I hope you didn't believe her."

"None of my business, anymore."

A shudder of humiliation ran through me. "Yeah, bad timing, though. If things had worked out between us, I would've had a chance to prove her wrong."

She twirled a piece of hair between her fingers. "Or right."

I opened my mouth to interject, but closed it again. When she looked at me, she was practically basking in the knowledge of her power over me. "Jesus, Peter, I'm kidding. It's a joke. Mallory was angry. I certainly didn't take anything she said to heart. I'm sure she's said loads of things about me to people when I've made her angry."

It did little to calm my insecurities. The corner of my mouth twitched. "Well," I said with a deep breath, "I guess we'll never know now." My tone carried a lightness I didn't actually feel.

"I guess not..."

There was a long, brittle silence, making our close proximity seem even more uncomfortable.

"Probably for the best anyway," I said.

She nodded. "I agree."

"And now, you've got ole Nintendo 64 to keep you company."

The tension melted between us as she furrowed her brow. "Nintendo 64?"

I laughed. "It's the only Link I could think of." When no recognition registered on her face, I added, "You never played..." I trailed off as she shook her head. "Well, now I know why it didn't work out between us."

"Why's that?"

"You're actually lame."

She threw her head back with a laugh. "Oh I am, am I?"

"I'm afraid so." I winced. "It's likely terminal. I'm afraid there's nothing we can do."

She nudged me playfully, her eyes twinkling with mischief. "You're such a dork." Our eyes connected, and for just the moment, she seemed to forget to blink, her gaze trained on mine. The tension was back, but of a different variety.

I spoke softly, trying not to break the spell we'd both fallen under. "We could've been something great, couldn't we? If we'd gotten the timing right."

Her chest rose and fell with a heavy breath, and she gave me a pained stare. "Maybe so."

I leaned forward ever so slightly, knowing with every bone and every nerve in my body it was the wrong thing to do. I didn't even want to do it, really, but I needed to prove something to myself. And to her. She didn't budge, watching me lean closer, and when I was nearly there, our lips nearly connected, my phone buzzed.

I jerked back, grateful for the interruption. Kissing Gina would be a mistake.

"I'm so sorry," I said.

At the same time, she said, "We shouldn't."

I lifted my phone, checking the screen as a tingle swept across the back of my neck.

M

I opened the message, my breathing slowing.

"What is it?"

"Oh, nothing..." I whispered, so low I wasn't sure she could hear me. So low I wasn't sure I'd even said it aloud.

I read over the text again, the tension releasing from my shoulders instantaneously. It included a link to a hotel downtown. Was it possible? Had I really found her?

She's in room 408. Wait for me... I have a plan.

CHAPTER TWENTY-SEVEN

AINSLEY

"**A**re you being good for your Aunt Glennon and Uncle Seth?" It was one of the only times I'd been away from all three of them for more than a night, and the distance was starting to bother me. I missed my children.

More than ever, I wanted to be with them. To be sure they were safe.

"Yes, Mom," Maisy said with a playful groan.

"And how about your brothers? Are you guys having fun?"

"Yeah, we went to the Molly Brown House yesterday. It was really cool. Aunt Glennon said she's going to take us to the botanical garden tomorrow too, if the weather clears up."

"That sounds really nice, sweetheart."

"When are you coming to get us, though? I miss you. Bailey and Janessa have been texting me like crazy. They've been together all fall break."

"I know. Hopefully I'll be able to get there soon. I just want to be sure you're all having fun." I didn't tell her they weren't coming home. Not yet.

"Uncle Seth bought me the new Karen McManus book. I can't wait to tell Dad about it."

Her words were an ice pick to my chest. Would she ever get to tell her father anything again? "Oh, that was nice of him," I squeaked out.

A knock on the door interrupted my conversation. I stood from the bed, checking the time. It was just after six, and I wasn't expecting anyone.

"Yeah, Jennessa said it's even better than the first, which is, like...impossible, and—"

"Honey, I'm so sorry. I have to go, okay? I'll call you back." I kept my voice low, ending the call and dropping the phone on the bed before making my way across the room. I pressed my face to the door, peering out. When I saw who was waiting for me, my chest tightened.

"Matt?" I swung open the door, looking down the hall to be sure we were alone. "What are you doing here?"

"Sorry. I would've called, but I didn't have your number, and... I guess I could've tried to call the hotel, huh? Hindsight, I guess. Um, sorry. I'm rambling. Is...is now a bad time?" He crossed his arms, then uncrossed them, shoving his hands into his pockets.

"Um, depends on what you need, I guess."

His smile was nervous. "I just thought...well, maybe we don't have to call it a date, you know? Like, maybe we can just call it hanging out or whatever. I mean, you gotta be bored just hanging out in a hotel room. Let's go grab coffee. Or a burger. My treat." He ran a hand over his hair. "I know what it's like to be in a not-so-good place, and you seem like you could really use the company. I know I could. I don't really know anyone in town, so..." He looked around. "And feel free to tell me to leave you alone if I'm overstepping. I'm not trying to...whatever. I'd just really like to get to talk to you a little more, if you'd like that. No complications. No commitments. Just dinner."

I forgot what I was planning to say the longer he spoke, all the reasons we shouldn't do it suddenly fading away. It was just dinner, after all. What was the harm in it? Maybe it would be nice to spend time outside of my own head for once. And I couldn't deny my curiosity.

I wouldn't cross a line.

I swore to myself I wouldn't—

"I can see you're thinking about it, so the salesman in me has to try and sell you on one final point here: it's a beautiful night, and a woman like you shouldn't be so alone. I know you think I'm too young for you, but all I'm proposing is an hour. Food, drinks, maybe a light joke peppered in now and again. If you hate it, feel free to never speak to me afterward." He lowered his head ever so slightly, so he was closer to my face. "But something tells me you won't hate it."

I chewed my bottom lip thoughtfully, then gave a resigned nod. What could it hurt? If nothing else, it would be a nice distraction for the evening. Nothing more. Matt was a nice guy. It was just dinner. "Okay, fine. You've convinced me."

"Yeah?"

"Yeah."

He clapped his hands together once. "All right. Do you need to change or anything?"

I looked down at the sweatpants and T-shirt I was wearing, not exactly ready for a hot date. But it wasn't a date. And, if I changed, that meant accepting that I wanted it to be more than I could allow it to be. "I'm good."

"Great!" he said, his voice an octave higher than it had been. "Excellent. Let's go."

"Let me grab my purse and shoes." I stepped back, crossing the room to slide into my shoes. I shoved my phone into my purse before checking the mirror long enough to run a comb through my hair. I still wasn't used to seeing my reflection.

He stayed in the hall, holding the door open but not invading my space without an invitation, which I was not planning to give him.

Once I was ready, we made our way down the hallway side by side. He kept watching me out of the corner of his eye, a wry grin on his lips, and when I'd catch him, he'd look away guiltily.

Even as I went, I felt ridiculous. I didn't understand my own fascination with the kid. Because that's what he was—a child. Just a handful of years older than Dylan. So, why was I letting myself be captivated by his frat-boy charm and winning smile? He wasn't exactly my type. The confidence he exuded, the sheer joy in his personality, was so far opposite from what I'd gotten with Peter. Maybe that was the appeal.

For an hour, with my new hair and my new life, I could pretend to be someone else.

We made it outside into the parking garage, and he held my door open for me, shutting it carefully after I was inside.

On our way out of the garage, he spoke finally, "So, any preferences?"

"Your choice."

"Fair enough... Are you thinking fast food or a restaurant?"

I pulled my shirt away from my chest, staring down at the small stain near the hem. Why hadn't I wanted to change, again? "Fast food, I guess." My stomach growled at the thought. I wasn't sure how long it had been since I'd eaten. "I'm starving."

"Fast food it is." He bobbed his head back and forth, turning right. "So, tell me about yourself."

"Why don't you tell me about yourself first?" I pressed.

He switched lanes, the muscle in his bicep twitching in a way that made me wonder if he was flexing. I looked away.

"Well, what do you want to know?"

"What brought you to Nashville?"

"That's an easy one. Work."

"What do you do? You're not in banking anymore, right?"

"You remembered?" He seemed pleased. "I'm a nurse, actually. I worked at a bank to get me through school, and I just graduated. A buddy of mine works at a hospital here. He put in a good word."

I couldn't deny the shock I felt. "A nurse? That's impressive."

"Thanks. It's no big deal. What about you? What do you do at the bank?"

"I..." Truth was, I didn't know anymore. Did I even still have a job? "I'm a manager."

"Oh, nice. That's crazy." We were both quiet for a moment. Then, he asked, "So, what are you escaping from in that hotel room?"

I paused, trying to decide what to tell him. Not the truth.

"Too personal?" he asked, interrupting my internal contemplation.

"Maybe just a little."

"Okay, cool. No worries. Um"—he clicked his tongue —"let's see, how about something simple: what's your favorite movie?"

"*The Proposal*," I said without having to think.

"Which one's that?"

"Sandra Bullock and Ryan Reynolds. It's a rom-com, you probably haven't—"

"Oh my god, the one with Betty White, right?" He chuckled. "Classic."

"What about you? Favorite movie?" It felt nice, losing ourselves in meaningless conversation. If I was being honest, it felt nice to talk to someone. Anyone. It felt like I'd been alone for so long.

"Hm, it's hard to say. I'm more of a TV guy. I really liked *Lost*."

"I haven't seen that."

"It's good." Every silence was heavy and weighted, filled with awkwardness as we both fought to fill it with small talk. "So, what about your kids? You have...how many?"

"Three."

"Wow." He scratched his chin. "How old are they?"

"Are you trying to decide how old I am?"

He shrugged a shoulder. "Not really, no. That doesn't matter to me."

"They're teenagers, well the boys are. Maisy, the one you met, she's eleven...going on thirty," I said finally with a nervous grin.

"Okay, I'm going to pull my first douchebag card of the night and say you do *not* look old enough to have teenagers."

I grinned despite the fact I was pretty sure he'd just called me old in a roundabout way. "Your *first* card? How many will there be?"

"I'll try to keep them to a minimum." He smirked, pointing up ahead as we neared a restaurant. "Is this okay?"

"This is perfect," I told him, so relieved to see food I wanted to leap from the truck.

"You're pretty cool, Ainsley, you know that? Not what I expected."

"What do you mean?"

"I mean, don't take this the wrong way, but when I first met you, I never expected you to be the kind of girl who'd be down for sweats and a drive-through meal as a first date... That level of chill is nice, ya know?"

"I thought this wasn't a date?"

He shrugged one shoulder. "Maybe I'll get you to reconsider."

I looked away, hiding the embarrassing way I was enjoying his attention. This hair dye was getting to my head, rewiring my mental responses. Something. This was not like me.

Once we had our food, he parked in a parking garage near the river front and we crossed the street, walking down the concrete steps to find a spot on the grass. The area was mostly quiet, except for a man playing guitar for a small crowd and a group of older women sitting idly reading the same book.

"So what do you think of Nashville?" I asked, running my hands over my knees to ease the chill in the air.

"I'm...still deciding."

"Oh, yeah?"

"It's warmer than I would like and I'm not crazy about your roads, but no state tax is cool and...the company isn't bad either." He nudged me playfully.

"The heat will be gone soon, but I-24 potholes are here to stay, I'm afraid."

He laughed. "I think they're going to have to start renting them out. What is the deal with that?"

I stared at him for a moment too long.

"What?" he asked.

"You're just...different than I imagined."

"You stole my line."

I rolled my eyes. "I'm serious."

"What did you think I was like?"

"Well"—I licked a bit of ketchup from my finger, placing my burger down—"when I first met you, I thought you were young and cocky and trying to hit on my preteen daughter."

He nearly choked, speaking with his mouth full. "What?"

"And then, I thought you must be some gold digger after my mother's money." I giggled when his eyes grew even wider.

"Man, I have *got* to work on my first impressions," he said, swiping the back of his hand across his forehead.

"Well, if it makes you feel any better, it had everything to do with my own issues and nothing to do with you. You've been incredibly kind to me. And my mother. So...thank you for that."

"Oh, it's no big deal," he said, waving me off. "I haven't really done anything."

"You have. You fixed my flat tire and my mother's fence, and you delivered my things today. Plus you got me out of the hotel tonight."

"Well, yeah, but that was for my own selfish reasons." He winked.

"Selfish or not, it was what I needed, so thank you."

He nodded, taking another bite of his burger, then putting on his best Southern accent, he said, "I'm glad to be of service, ma'am."

"Oh, god." I covered my nose. "Leave that accent to the experts, and please don't call me ma'am."

"You just accused me of being a pedophile and a sugar baby all in one sentence. I think you deserve it," he said playfully.

"Fair enough." I lay back on the grass, staring up at the sky with a loud puff of air.

After a few moments, he lay down next to me. "For the record, I did offer to help your mom both of those times because I was hoping for a chance to see you again, so you aren't wrong about me having romantic intentions. You were just assuming I was after the wrong girl."

I turned my head slightly to look at him. "*Romantic* intentions, hm?"

"We're lying in the grass looking at the stars," he said with a chuckle, then jutted his chin toward the guitar player down the hill from us. "There's even music playing. I think we're putting Ryan and Sandra to shame."

Warmth spread through my stomach and out to my extremities, my breathing growing shallow.

"It's killing me not to kiss you right now," he whispered, a wistful smile growing on his lips.

I couldn't bring myself to say anything, for fear whatever I said might be an encouragement for him to do so. I couldn't trust myself. What was I doing? Why was I here? What was I thinking?

There were so many more important things.

"But I think I'll save that for our first date." Without a word, he turned his face back toward the sky, the corners of his mouth fighting against a smile, and left me to ponder my racing thoughts.

CHAPTER TWENTY-EIGHT

PETER

I approached the front desk of the hotel, worriedly scratching my head and patting my pockets a bit overzealously. The young man behind the counter watched me with an apathetic stare, pushing the bridge of his glasses up farther on his nose.

"Can I help you?"

"Actually, yes. This is so embarrassing, but I've lost my room key somewhere, and I left my phone in the room. Could I get a spare?"

"Sure." He looked relieved I wasn't asking him to do something difficult as he typed something into the computer in front of him and asked, "What's your room number?"

"It's 408."

He typed it in before eyeing my bandaged wrist suspiciously. I dropped my arm to my side. "Name?"

"Greenburg. It's probably under my wife's name, Ainsley."

He nodded slowly, his eyes skimming the screen. "Do you have some ID?"

I produced my wallet in a flash, a carefree smile on my lips. "Of course. Thank you for asking."

"No problem." He half glanced at the ID and spun around, using one of the keys on his wrist to unlock a cabinet. Seconds later, he was handing me a new room key.

"Thanks. Uh, is there any charge?"

"Nah," he said, rubbing a finger across the pimple on his chin. "You're good."

"Thanks, man." I turned away from him and headed for the elevators, my body trembling with adrenaline.

I was so close.

So close.

The excitement was almost too much.

When I reached her room, I stood still for a moment, listening to be sure she was indeed gone. To make sure he'd taken her away like we'd planned. After a few moments, I pressed the key to the door and watched the light flash green. I turned the handle, waiting again as the seconds passed.

One...

Two...

On three, I pushed the door open and rushed inside, shutting it behind me and pressing my back to the door.

"Hello?" I called.

No answer.

I moved farther into the room, spying her open suitcase on the end of the bed. I picked up a T-shirt, lifting it to my nose and drawing in a breath. I sorted through the bag, filled only with her wrinkled clothing and toiletries.

I looked around, bending down to check the floor and underneath the bed. Where were the children's bags?

I checked the bathroom, searching for any sign of their things—toothbrushes, clothes, anything, but there was nothing.

Next, I checked the mini-fridge.

No soda.

No bags of chips on the desk.

The small silver trash can only contained a few used tea bags and the unopened bag of chocolate-covered peanuts I'd bought her. Next to the bed, there were two plastic bags of snacks, a romance book Maisy would've never read, and two coloring books. Were these for the kids? I hadn't seen them color in years...

It was obvious what was going on.

They were either staying in another room or they weren't staying there at all.

Where did they go, Ainsley?

I moved back into the bathroom, looking around. In the trash can, there was a green box. *What the...*

I picked it up cautiously.

No.

Hair dye?

She couldn't be serious. She wouldn't have ever actually dyed her hair. This had to be for something else. Ainsley's red hair was...part of her. It was special. Beautiful. It was one of my favorite things about her. How could she even consider changing it?

I felt as if I might be sick as I threw the box back into the trash with disgust.

How dare she?

How *dare* she?

I stalked from the bathroom. Next to the door, there was an armoire. I made my way toward it and pulled it open. Inside, there were hangers, plastic bags for dry cleaning, and an ironing board. I stepped inside of the space, trying to determine if there was enough room for me to hide.

I shuffled things around, shoving the ironing board to the opposite end and pushing the hangers over with it. Doing that gave me just enough room to shut the door and bathe myself in total darkness.

I pulled out my phone and checked the time.

Now, we wait...

NEARLY AN HOUR PASSED before I heard the first sign of their return. Her voice carried from down the hall in the form of a laugh. She sounded happy. Carefree.

Wasn't that just the story of my life?

She was happy, and I was hidden in a closet trying to fix our marriage.

I heard the lock disengage and the door open, and I held my breath, incredibly aware of how close she was.

"Thank you for doing this...for convincing me," she said. I grimaced. *Oh, shut up.*

"I had a really nice time," he said. I pressed my eye to

the crack in the door, trying to see whether he'd come inside with her. From there, I could just make out the muddy brown of her hair. Rage bubbled in my belly. This little tantrum had gone too far. How stupid was she going to feel once things had blown over and she still had to live with that color for months?

"Yeah?"

"Yeah. And I'd like to do it again, if you're up for it. When you're done escaping, I mean."

Escaping? Where the fuck did she think she was going?

"I can't believe I'm going to say this, but I'd like that."

I shoved my hands in my pockets to keep myself from lunging out of the armoire right then. Who did she think she was?

"Okay, cool."

Cool? Calm the fuck down, tough guy.

"Um...do you want to come inside?"

What the... No. No, he doesn't want to come inside. No, he doesn't want to—

"Uh, I'd better not."

"Oh, right, I—"

"It's not that I don't want to," he said quickly. Too quickly. "Believe me, I want to."

We believe you, all right. Don't even think about it.

"I just want to be respectful."

Respectful? Who was this guy? The fucking Pope?

"I know you're in a weird place, and I don't want to rush things. But I'd like to see you again. I have an early shift tomorrow. Maybe I could come by after."

She rebounded quickly, unfazed. "Sure."

"Awesome. I, uh... Well, all that waiting for the first date talk, I'm not sure I have the willpower for that."

She giggled, the sound interrupted by a worse noise. I slapped a hand to my mouth as I heard the sloppy, disgusting soundtrack of their kiss.

He was kissing her. The fucker was actually kissing her.

"I would've kicked myself if I didn't at least do that."

I'll be happy to do the kicking for you.

"I'll see you tomorrow, Matt."

"I'll see you then. Good night, Ainsley."

The hell you will.

After another brief pause, the door shut and I heard her back slide against it, releasing a lovesick sigh that sent ice to my core. What did she have to be so happy about? Peering through the crack, I watched her slide her shoes off and run a hand through her ridiculous hair. With a smile like a schoolgirl who'd just been asked out by the prom king, she shook her head and moved forward, past my hiding place.

I pulled the syringe out of my pocket, holding it at the ready, and shoved the door open before she'd had time to process the sound.

"Peter?" she cried as I lunged forward, blinded by my rage. I jabbed the needle into her neck just as she'd done to me so many times in the past.

I jerked my arm back. "Sorry to ruin your evening."

Her hand went to her neck, then she pulled it away

as if looking for blood. She stepped back, searching for the phone in her hand, already dazed and disoriented.

"What did you do?" she cried, slurring her words. I plucked the phone from her grasp, but she didn't seem to notice, still searching.

"It works fast, doesn't it?" I asked, clicking my tongue. "It'll be lights out soon, don't worry."

She jerked forward with determination, grabbing the landline phone from the nightstand, but I tore it from her grasp with ease, my pulse pounding in my ears. "Just give in to it, Ains. It's easier that way."

"Fuck...you..." she whispered, trying to push herself up from the floor, though she was sinking faster than she seemed to realize.

I cracked my knuckles, the corners of my mouth playing into a grimace. "Maybe another time. I'm pretty tired. Although, lover boy seemed pretty happy to try. Too bad you're going to have to cancel your plans tomorrow night."

She wasn't listening, too busy trying to stand up, and then, without warning, she opened her mouth and screamed with everything she had left in her. I clapped a hand over her lips in an instant, ending the noise.

A second later, she went limp in my arms.

There now, that wasn't so bad, was it? Let's get you home.

CHAPTER TWENTY-NINE

AINSLEY

When I awoke, I instantly knew something was wrong, though my mind was dense with fog, only bits and pieces of memories coming back to me. Voices, smells, images.

The kids.

Grass.

Music.

A stained shirt.

A stained carpet.

Everything hurt. Nothing made sense.

Where was I?

Why was it so cold?

Why were my arms—

Tied. My arms were tied. I was tied down to something.

Panic shot through me like a bolt of lightning. I struggled against the strength of the material binding me as I tried to make sense of it all, tried to clear my blurry vision and ease my pounding head.

As I began to find focus, I realized the issues with my vision weren't due to whatever was wrong. I couldn't see because it was dark. Pitch black. We were either moving, or my head was spinning.

Then, the smell hit me.

The dank, cool air.

The musty smell.

The darkness.

I recalled the darkness most of all.

No.

Not so long ago, I'd tiptoed across this room and slit the throat of a woman my husband intended to kill. Watching him take in the fact that he'd never get the pleasure—never get to be her whole world—was one of the joys I would take to my grave.

Now, I had to wonder if that grave would come sooner than I'd hoped.

Would I be just another body buried in the woods soon enough? Just another victim rotting under a concrete patio? Once, I could say with certainty he'd never hurt me. Now, though, all bets were off.

One of us was going to have to kill the other, and he clearly, as I struggled against the ropes that bound me, had the upper hand.

I jerked my arms and kicked my feet, trying to break free however I could. The chair scooted across the concrete floor, its rubber feet shrieking with each movement. As a last-ditch attempt, I leaned over, throwing all my weight to the side.

Again.

Again.

It tipped, but didn't fall.

Again.

Again.

Finally, it gave way, the chair leaning farther and farther to the right until—

CRASH.

I landed with a thud on the ground, my head cracking against the concrete with dizzying force. My arm had been smashed under the weight of it all and, if it wasn't broken, it was very badly wounded.

I winced, trying to catch the breath the impact had knocked out of me. My eyes beaded with tears, but I blinked them away.

Not today.

You have to be strong today.

I had to be strong for my children. Had to get out for them. Had to save them. Ignoring the searing pain in my arm, I tugged against the fabric—up and down, right and left, until the rope burned my wrists. It wasn't working. I wiggled in place as I tried and failed to break the metal chair.

There had to be another way.

Think.

Think.

Think.

With a deep breath, I pulled my right leg over,

despite the pain as the chair pinched my arm again, leaning farther and farther until I could turn myself over. Face-first on the concrete, I slid across the floor, no doubt tearing the top layer of skin from my cheeks and nose. I stopped, catching my breath and swallowing down vomit, momentarily easing the pain, and started again.

The concrete burned, my entire weight forcing my face harder into it. I shifted my legs one at a time, half an inch at a time, stopping only when the pain was entirely too much.

With my next move, I felt the rope wrapped around my calf moving lower. I pushed forward, feeling it budge just a bit more. I gave one final jerk, and the rope slid to my ankle. I stopped, breathing a sigh of relief and trying to control my trembling.

I fell to my side again with a loud CLANG, panting and shaking, the pain in my face so unbearable I was sure I was going to pass out. I closed my eyes, twisting my ankle slowly and pulling my heel up until I felt it slip through the hole.

I was free.

At least, one leg was free.

My chest felt as if it might explode from happiness. Blood dripped into my eye, and I squeezed it shut, moving my toes to grab hold of the other cloth and pull them down my opposite leg. My knees throbbed, but I couldn't stop. Couldn't quit trying, not even for a second.

I had no idea when Peter would be back or what his plan was. Getting myself free and escaping through the emergency exit was my only choice.

Finally, I pulled my heel up through the hole and my second leg was free. I kicked them with triumph, my heart drumming in my chest. Rolling forward once again, my head screamed for relief, and, using all of my strength, I was able to stand. The weight of the chair made balancing myself impossible. I swayed, slamming into the wall, then turned.

With my back to the wall, I scrubbed my wrists up and down it, using as much force as I could to get the rope to tear. I winced and cried and bit my lip and fought against every nerve in my body screaming for me to stop, and finally...finally, I felt it rip. The rope broke free and the chair fell to the ground in an instant. I gathered my bleeding arms at my chest, sure the pain would never stop, and began to spin around, searching for a way out.

There was no sign of light in the room by design, so I had no idea what time of day or night it was. No idea if Peter would be home or if he'd be waiting for me. I thought back to the text message he'd sent me, to the picture of the blueprint. If I remembered correctly, the exit was on the far-left wall. But which way was left? Which way was I facing?

I put my hands out, feeling along the room, searching for anything to help orient me. My fingers ran across a shelf full of tools. Weapons, maybe. Then something lower—textured, cool to the touch. A freezer. I pulled my hands away in a hurry and spun around, slamming into something.

Some*one*.

"Going somewhere?" His breath hit my face, his

hands gripping my arms, and I jerked away, colliding with the shelf of tools. I felt for one as he grabbed hold of my wrist, his fingers sticky in my blood, but he didn't seem to notice.

I skimmed my hand across the shelf with panic, grabbing onto the first solid thing I could find—a metal tape measure—and slamming it against his jaw.

He released me. "What the fuck?"

I ran across the room, feeling desperately against the wall for a way out.

Please.

Please.

Please.

Please.

Please.

Nothing budged. It was all solid. All concrete. There was no way out. No escape.

Except there was. I needed to stay calm. I needed to keep myself together. This was what I did. In the worst circumstances, I'd always managed to pull through when it mattered most. This was no different.

Across the room, I could hear him moving around, making no effort to be quiet in his search for me.

"Where'd you go?" he shouted, pounding the shelf against the wall. Tools clattered to the ground. I kept myself against the wall, feeling for any sort of groove or loose brick. It had to be there. It had to.

The light flicked on—too bright, too sudden. I squeezed my eyes shut, wincing and ducking my head as my vision clouded with specks.

"Well, aren't you a sight for sore eyes," he said dryly. I rubbed my eyes, spying him walking toward me. He shoved the freezer, pinning me between it and the wall in the corner with nowhere to go.

When he reached me, looking entirely too pleased with himself, he pressed his finger into my cheek.

The pain was what I imagined an electric fence felt like, or a white-hot poker branding your skin.

I cried out, jerking my face away from him.

Unfazed, he stared at the blood, then pressed his finger to his lips, closing his eyes with pleasure. "You always did taste sweet." When he opened his eyes, he ran his tongue over his teeth, enjoying the torment. I turned away, refusing to look at him. Was this the face his victims saw? Was this the last image in their minds before he murdered them?

"You won't get away with this," I told him, my face throbbing so badly I could hardly move my mouth.

"Oh, but I will."

"You won't find them," I said, smiling through the pain. "You won't ever find them. Not without me. If you kill me, our kids are gone forever. They'll live their lives knowing you were a monster."

He clicked his tongue. "Unlikely, but I guess it's a risk I'll have to take, hm?" He stepped closer, a darkness flickering in his eyes. An emptiness. I looked down. "It didn't have to come to this, Ains. It really, really didn't. All I wanted was to start over. To fix things. But you were too busy acting like you're a saint. Newsflash, baby, there are no saints in this marriage. We're both murderers." He leaned back, smiling wickedly and grabbing my face, forcing me to look at him. I glanced down at his bandaged wrist, fighting the urge to smile as I recalled biting him. "It just turns out one of us is a little better at it than the other."

"Well, practice makes perfect, doesn't it?" I asked through bared teeth.

"Unfortunately for you, it does."

It was then I saw the weapon in his opposite hand. A knife, held out to the side. He lifted it up, shaking his head. "I hate that you've made me do thi—"

"I'm pregnant!" I shouted, a hand over my stomach protectively.

He dropped the knife, stepping back. "Y-you're—"

"I'm pregnant. I just found out. It's early, but it's true."

He shook his head. "It's impossible."

"It's not. Go buy a test. I'll prove it."

His face wrinkled with contemplation. "You weren't going to tell me?"

"We aren't exactly in a good place, Peter. I was still deciding if I wanted to keep it."

"And you weren't going to include me in that decision?"

"I'm including you now."

"*Because you're about to die,*" he said, scoffing, using his opposite hand to rub his bandaged wrist. The gauze he'd used to wrap it looked dirty and in need of changing.

"No matter the reason, I'm telling you. I'm pregnant. If you kill me, you'll have to kill me knowing that."

When he looked back at me, his eyes glistened with tears. "Another baby?"

I chewed my lip, nodding.

"D-do the kids know?"

"No one knows but me. And now you."

He bent over, picking up the knife, both hands held up in surrender. "I don't want to hurt you. I never wanted to hurt you. But...what choice do I have?"

"I'm offering you a choice right now."

"I'm listening." He crossed his arms.

"I'll come home. I'll bring the kids home. We...we can try again. Start over and fix this. It's...it's not going to be easy." I kept my eyes trained on the knife in his hands as he shifted. "It's not going to be easy, okay? But when have we ever had things easy? We can do this, right? Because you were right...I do love you. And you love me. It's why you haven't killed me, isn't it? You could've done it before I was able to fight back, but you didn't. You waited." I paused. "You waited because, as much as we may hate each other sometimes, we love each other more."

He cocked his head to the side, his eyes darting back and forth between mine as if trying to decide whether or not to trust me. "I want proof that you're pregnant."

"Done. But I want something in return."

"What?"

"I need to know where the bodies are, Peter."

"Why? So you can turn me in again?"

"No, so I can protect myself. If you have them hidden, you could just as easily frame me."

The corner of his mouth twitched and my suspected

plan was confirmed. "We can't make this work unless you tell me where they are."

He seemed to contemplate it. "Maybe I could tell you where *one* is, but not yet."

"When?"

"Patience," he said. "I need to make sure you're all in. Let's handle the test first. Then we'll get the kids home, and then *maybe* I'll tell you. If you prove your loyalty."

"No. That's not fair. The only way this works is if we both lay all our cards on the table. I need to know you're not going to double-cross me."

"And what protects me, then?"

"The kids," I said firmly. "I'll call and have the kids come home."

"Today?"

"Today."

He looked unconvinced, but finally took a step back, still gripping the knife. "Let's get you cleaned up first. They shouldn't see you like that. And, Ainsley, if you try anything, I will kill you. I won't hesitate. Please don't make me do that."

He pressed in the two bricks that opened the door from the inside and stepped out of the room, the fresh air as soothing as ice water on a hot day. I sucked it into my lungs as if it might keep me safe for just a moment longer.

He led me through the garage door and into the house. Near the bedroom, I breathed in the scent of the smoke. It was less potent than it had been, but still enough to give me a headache. It was a wonder Peter had been able to stay there. Although sometimes, when he was so in his head, it was a wonder he noticed anything at all.

"Get in the shower." He pointed toward the hallway. "I don't want them to see you this way."

I did as I was told, making my way down the hall with him following closely behind. I refused to let him see me cry or let him see me afraid. I had to keep it together no matter what.

"Can I have some privacy?" I asked, standing in front of the bathroom door.

"Privacy from your husband? I don't think so." He reached around me and shoved the door open. "Come on."

Once inside, I removed my clothes with shaking hands, turning away from him in an attempt to shield myself. He made no move to look away, nor any apologies that it had to be this way. In fact, I was pretty sure he was enjoying every moment of it.

In the shower, I washed myself slowly, the water painful against my many wounds. With my clothes off, I could see the bruises and scrapes on my knees, some older and some newer. Had I tried to escape before? Could I not remember it?

Or maybe the bruises were from the fall I'd taken at the hotel. I couldn't be sure. I scrubbed my hair with cautious movements, every twist or turn of my wrists felt as if it was tearing the wounds open again. I touched my face gingerly under the water, trying to assess the extent of the damage.

"Almost done?" Peter asked, when I'd apparently

been taking too long. The shape of him was blurry through the shower door, but still, I could see the knife in his hands.

I actively fought to stop the thoughts that told me I caused this. That this was my fault, and if I'd walked away all those years ago, I wouldn't be here.

I'd chosen my fate. Chosen to accept what my husband was and believe he could never be a monster to me. I chose to believe I was the exception, but we're never really the exception, are we? None of us.

I'd stayed with him for the children, believing it was in their best interest that we stay together. Now, it was as if the curtain had been lifted and I could see every mistake I'd made along the way. Every wrong turn.

I could see my future—a future with Peter. A future of fear.

It wasn't what I wanted. There was no doubt in my mind anymore. I had to end this, I had to protect the kids, but I wasn't sure I could do it. The fixer in me was giving up. Shutting down. She was tired, angry, burned out.

He handed me a towel when I shut off the water, and I patted my body dry, wrapping it around myself. "I can't believe you did that to your hair."

I ignored him. "Did you bring my clothes home?"

"I had to empty your suitcase in the hotel room to get you here."

I ignored the fact that my husband had just told me he stuffed my unconscious body into a suitcase in order to lock me in a murder room and shuffled past him. "Did all of my stuff get burned in the fire?"

"No. Most of it's fine. I threw out what was ruined and fixed the bed. I shampooed the carpet and I might have to repaint the ceiling, but other than that, you'd never know."

I pushed open the bedroom door, the smoke smell overwhelming me, and began coughing. He crossed the room, opening a window. "It's been closed up for a few days... I've been sleeping on the couch, waiting for...for you to come home." He opened the closet and pulled out a pair of jeans and a T-shirt. "Here, will these work?"

I opened my drawer and grabbed a bra and under-wear, hardly paying attention to the clothes he'd handed me as I slid them on. "Now what?"

"Brush your hair. Where are the kids? We'll go pick them up."

I dug in the drawer of my vanity, pulling out a comb and running it through my hair quickly. "Don't you want me to take the test first? I thought you'd want to go get it."

"We can do that on the way."

I paused, thinking. There went that plan for escape.

"Well? Where are they?" he demanded, growing impatient.

"They're with Glennon," I admitted, my voice low.

"Glennon? What, in Canada?"

"No, they're home for a while."

"Oh. So, they're at Glennon's house? I was just there looking for you."

"They haven't been there long. Glennon and Seth just came home yesterday," I said. "To watch the kids. I should call and tell her we're on the way. Do you have my phone?"

He dug in his pocket and pulled it out, handing it to me and moving to stand closer. "Don't...don't try anything stupid, okay?"

His tone had changed. He almost did sound regretful now.

I turned the phone on, ignoring the voicemails I had from work and Glennon, and opened my texts. "I'll just send her a message."

He nodded, watching me closely.

I opened my contacts and tapped **G**, typing out a quick message: **I'm with Peter. We're coming to pick up the kids today. Want to meet us at the park by my house?**

"Why the park?" Peter asked apprehensively, after I'd already pressed send.

"They were supposed to go there today. I don't want to ruin their plans."

He didn't look entirely convinced, but nodded in the direction of my screen. "She's typing."

My heart pounded in my chest, praying she'd understand.

See you in an hour.

I closed out of the message and slid my phone in my pocket, but Peter held out his hand. "Give it back to me."

"Don't you think the kids will think it's odd that you're holding my phone hostage?"

"We'll talk more once I've seen them." He shut the

phone off and shoved it in his pocket. "Let's go." He jutted his chin forward and we made our way down the hall, stopping only briefly for me to pull shoes on.

On the way to the park, I stared out the window, going over everything in my head.

"This really will be for the best," he said, sounding as if he were trying to convince himself as well as me. "For the kids." He reached his hand across the car, touching my stomach gently. "All of them." I tensed under his touch, refusing to move, and when he pulled his hand back, he added, "And for us, too."

I didn't respond.

"We're good together, Ains. I know you're having a hard time seeing it right now, but tensions are just high. It's a bad time. Couples go through bad times. Maybe we could try counseling again, when you're feeling up to it. Or...or maybe we could take some time off and travel. Maybe we'll do date nights again. We owe it to them to try, don't we? It's like you said...we own each other's sins. We know the deepest, darkest parts of each other. No one else will ever know you like I do. And no one will ever know me like you. We're meant to be together. You have to believe that." He was almost manic, his tone insistent and erratic. He needed me to believe him. He needed everything to be okay again so he could go back to his life of ruining ours.

I nodded. "You're right, Peter. You know everything about me, but it's not exactly fair because you're still holding this giant secret looming over my head. I've done my end of the bargain, but you still haven't told me where the bodies are. Shouldn't I be helping you hide them? Shouldn't I be making sure you've covered your tracks?"

"No offense, Ains, but I have a little more experience with this than you do. I've managed not to get caught yet."

"Barely," I mumbled.

"The one time I panicked was when it was Stefan, and that's because I wasn't prepared and he was a cop. And because I never wanted you to see me like that. It changed things. But the rest you can trust me with. And you can trust me with the secret. I'd never do anything to hurt you."

"You literally just tried to kill me."

"*You gave me no choice!*" he shouted, then lowered his voice. "I just want us to be together. I need that. *We* need that."

"What are you saying? You're never going to tell me?"

"They're safe, Ains. They're safe. That's all that matters."

"No, it's not all that matters," I shouted across the car at him. "You lied! You lied to me. After everything I've done for you."

"*For* me? You mean *to* me? You tried to kill me, Ainsley. You tried to turn me in. You think I don't know I need a little extra protection? I'm not stupid, okay?"

"So, what? You're just going to hold it over me forever? *Are you going to walk the dog, or do I need to make a call?*"

"What? Like you held everything over me, you mean? You ruined everything. Everything was perfect. I had these little...sections of my life. Everything stayed in its box. Everything was neat and tidy. And then you came along and you mixed everything up. And you brought all the boxes together until I had a mess. And now I have to clean up the mess that you made. So, yeah, I'm going to hold that over you if I have to. But if you're on your best behavior, I won't—"

"I'm not a child!" I bellowed. "You can't do this to me. You have to tell me. If you want mutual trust you have to tell me. Are they in the woods still? At least tell me that."

His lips pressed into a thin line. I watched for his cheeks to flame pink, but they didn't. He wasn't lying. Then again, he wasn't saying anything at all.

"Peter, please?" I lowered my voice. "Please just tell me. Please. It's going to drive me crazy."

"It's better if we go back to the way things were." His fingers gripped the steering wheel. "It's better if you're in the dark from here on out."

"You can't be serious."

"Oh, I am," he said. "Deadly." He chuckled to himself, making me feel sick, then turned up the radio. "Now, just relax. We're going to bring the kids home, and everything's going to be fine. You'll see." He took my hand, squeezing it so hard I yelped when I tried to pull away.

Twenty minutes later, we pulled into the main parking lot of our park, and he looked around. "Where is she?"

"I don't know. I don't have my phone."

He glared at me and opened his car door. "This had better not be a trick."

"How would it be a trick? You saw the text message."

I reached for my door, too, but he was faster. He pressed the button and locked me in. "Don't move. You don't want to scare them..." He gestured toward his face.

I bit down just as I saw her car pulling into the lot next to us. "There she is."

He saw the car as I spoke, his face growing ashen. "What the..."

Gina stepped out of her car, her phone in her hand. She saw me in the passenger seat, and I watched the horror flash in her eyes.

"What are you doing here, Gina?" Peter's voice was casual, as if this was all totally normal.

"Let her go," she said through gritted teeth.

"What are you talking about?"

"I know all about it, Peter. You're lucky I haven't called the cops yet."

"Called the cops? Why? What are you talking about?"

She'd reached my door then, and I unlocked it. He didn't try to stop me as I stepped out to stand next to her. "I should've known better when I saw you on that dating app. I should've seen you for what you are—a cheater, a liar, and an abuser."

"Abuser? Now, wait a minute... I'm not sure what she's told you, but Gina, you know me. You know I wouldn't... I mean... You know what she did to me." He held up his wrist, showing her the bandage.

I watched as he switched back and forth between anger and charm, the emotions flashing across his face like flashes of a camera, trying hard to convey his rage to me while still convincing Gina of his innocence.

"Save it," she cut him off. "Look at her face. Are you honestly going to tell me you didn't hurt her worse?"

I tucked my cheek into my shoulder. "Thank you for coming."

"Of course. I told you I would any time." She nodded, putting a hand on my shoulder. I winced, though it was one of the only parts of my body that wasn't sore.

"I'm confused..." Peter said. "What did she tell you?"

"I told her everything, Peter." I chose my moment to finally speak up. "How you've been cheating on me and abusing me for years. How I finally decided to leave you, but I've been worried you'd track me down."

"I called her when you came to the office asking for the corporate card after you'd been off for a few days. I knew something was up because you, like, never miss work. I've seen enough true crime documentaries to know when men start acting shady, it's usually for a reason. I knew you'd had problems in the past, so I called just to make sure she was okay. And she told me what you've done to her."

"Gina made me save her number and swear I'd call if I ever needed anything."

"And then I went with you when you were looking for her to make sure nothing happened." She rubbed my arm. "I would've called the cops if Ainsley hadn't begged me not to."

"For the children's sake," I added. "But now, Peter, it's over. I'm going to walk away, go with Gina, and take the kids far away. If you try to come after me, if you ever try to contact the kids, Gina will be my witness. She'll tell the cops everything. Maybe this time they'll believe me." I drove home the final point. Though I hadn't been able to get the answers I needed, I hoped this threat would be enough to keep him away from me for good.

"I already told Beckman everything," Gina said, "on my way over here. Ainsley won't press charges, so we'll respect her wishes, but we want you gone—"

He shook his head in horror. "It's my company—"

"Beckman's president. He outranks you. If we need to bring the rest of the partners in on this, we will. Trust me, I'd be happy to. But it's up to you."

He took a step back, glancing in the car, and I worried he'd try something stupid. There were people around. Witnesses. And Gina had already said she'd told Beckman our story. But still, Peter's impulses usually got the best of him.

"Let's go," I told Gina, urging her forward. When I looked back over my shoulder, Peter still looked dumbstruck, watching us move away from him.

He thought he'd won, but by some miracle, I'd managed my way out of it again.

"Thank you," I told her once more as we slid into our seats and buckled up.

"You're welcome. I'm glad you texted. Are you okay? We should really get you to the hospital. Those scrapes look really bad."

"I'll be okay. For now, I just want to get to my kids."

She didn't seem to agree with the plan, but didn't immediately argue. "Are you sure you don't want to go to the police? Guys like that...they don't usually give up without a fight."

"He put up a hell of a fight," I told her. "But going to the police will only hurt my children. I don't want them to know what a monster he is. I just want him to leave us alone."

She swallowed. "I get it. Really, I do. It's hard to recover from that... To know that part of you came from someone like him."

Something in her voice made me think she knew all too well what I was saying.

"But I want you to be careful. I never wanted to get you involved. He's dangerous, Gina. Unpredictable."

"You didn't force me to get involved. I inserted myself into the situation. I insisted you save my number. I wanted to help you, Ainsley. I'm not worried about Peter. I can take care of myself." She was quiet for a moment, though she looked like she had something she wanted to say. Finally, she spoke up. "I know this...this company. They helped my friend. *Mujer*. They help battered and abused women and kids. It's super secretive, but this woman and her husband who run it, they're great. I can put you in contact—"

"I'm okay," I promised, reaching out and putting a hand on her arm. "You've done more than enough. I'm going to go away. Take my kids and go. I'll be okay now, thanks to you."

She ran her tongue along her teeth. "Where will you go? Do you have family you can stay with, or..."

"I'll figure out something."

"Men like him don't deserve to get away with this."

"He's lost everything he cares about, Gina. His company, his marriage, his family. Peter may not be going to jail, but...there are worse things." I swallowed, stone-faced. The reality of it was bitter. It wasn't easy. Peter hadn't been wrong about how much I loved him, but that didn't change the fact that I loved my children more. "He'll be alone for the rest of his life." I paused. "I know you don't agree with my decision, but—"

"But it is *your* decision. And I respect it. Just... promise me you'll be careful. Wherever you go."

I smiled. "I will. I promise."

"So, where can I take you?"

I gave her directions to my mother's house, then rested my head against the window as she navigated us there, a pit in my stomach and throbbing in my head as I thought about the last time I'd told someone my husband was abusive. *Poor Stefan...*

That time, it had been to save my marriage.

This time, it was to save myself.

CHAPTER THIRTY

AINSLEY

The next morning, I awoke to the sound of a knocking on the door. My entire body ached, every movement as painful as if I'd been hit by a truck.

"You up?" Mom asked, pushing the door open and peering in.

"Yeah, I am," I lied, easing myself up off the bed.

"Do you want breakfast? What time's your flight?"

"Eleven," I told her. "And yeah, breakfast sounds nice." I stood and crossed the room. "Do you happen to have a toothbrush I can borrow?"

"Of course. Be right back." She left the room and reappeared moments later with a red plastic toothbrush still in its packaging. Passing it to me, she studied my face. "There's some antibiotic cream under the sink, too. The better care you take of it, the less chance it'll scar. And what a nasty scar that would be."

"Thanks, Mom."

She nodded. "I can't believe you ruined your hair like

that." I turned away from her, refusing to respond, and she went on. "Are you sure you're ready to travel? Why not stay here for a few days and rest?"

"I told you...I have to go get the kids. I only stayed behind to take care of things."

"And everything's taken care of now?"

"Yep." In the bathroom, I spread toothpaste on the brush and placed it in my mouth.

"Are you sure you shouldn't see some sort of specialist? I mean, it just looks awful." She was still eyeing the scrape.

I spit, lifting back up to say, "Well, it's from a car accident, so it's not going to look great. I'll be fine. Just a little road rash."

A doorbell rang out downstairs, and she twisted her mouth in thought. "Are you expecting anyone?"

I thought of Gina, who'd dropped me off the night before. We hadn't made plans to meet up again, but it was entirely possible she'd come back. Then, without warning, my heart plummeted, worrying it was Peter.

No.

No.

It wasn't him. It couldn't be.

Would it always be that way? Would I worry every phone call or doorbell for the rest of my life would be him?

I shuddered. "I don't think so."

"I'll get it. There are some of your old clothes still in the dresser. You'll probably still fit in them."

Ignoring her underhanded comment, I dug through

the drawers, pulling out a pair of jeans and a sweatshirt to cover the scrapes on my wrists. It was going to be bad enough flying with my face as banged up as it was. I didn't need to give anyone any further reason to notice me.

Once I'd gotten dressed and brushed my hair, I made my way down the stairs. Halfway down, I could hear my mother's laughter from the kitchen. I rounded the corner and gasped at the sight of Matt, who looked equally horrified to see me.

Or rather, to see my face in its current state.

"Jesus, what happened?" He moved toward me quickly, his hands outstretched as he examined the wound. He examined me with such tenderness, I suddenly felt tears stinging my eyes.

"Car accident." I carried on the lie I'd told my mother and the one I'd tell my children as I pulled out of his grasp.

"When? Is that where you were last night? I came by your hotel room, but I thought maybe you'd gotten freaked out because...well...because of what happened." He cast a wary glance over his shoulder, obviously trying to decide if I'd told my mother about our night together, though at that point, it was the least of my concerns.

"No, I'm sorry. I wasn't standing you up. I was in an accident and came here after. I completely forgot about—"

"Sure. Yeah..." He was still studying me with a pained expression. "My gosh... It looks really bad. Did you go to the hospital? You could have a concussion. I can drive you if you want."

I waved off his concern. "I'm fine. It was minor."

"Ainsley, I know I have no right to tell you what to do, but as a medical professional, I feel like I need to insist that you go get checked out. You have a pretty serious road rash. Were you thrown from a vehicle? That doesn't sound minor."

"I'm fine, I swear. It looks worse than it feels."

"Do you think she'll be scarred, Matt? Will it heal okay?" Mom asked from across the room.

"It's hard to say," he admitted, still scrutinizing me. He moved the collar of my shirt and lifted my chin with his finger, checking my neck to see where the wounds ended. I pulled away self-consciously.

"I swear I'm—"

Mom's phone began to ring from where it lay on the counter, and she picked it up, looking at the caller ID. "Oh, honey, it's Glennon. Want to take it?"

I'd never in my life heard my mother call me honey, but I reached for the phone anyway. "Hello?"

When I'd returned to the house without a phone, I'd called Glennon to let her know what was going on and arranged for her to pick me up from the airport this evening. She'd been worried sick after my abrupt hang up on Maisy, and I imagined she'd be calling me frequently until I arrived.

"Ainsley, I—I don't know what happened. He was here and then he was gone, and it all happened so fast and he must've gotten ahold of a credit card, but I don't know how because I'm always so careful with my cards and Seth never leaves his wallet out and—"

"Wait, what?" I interrupted, trying to make sense of her frazzled words. "What are you talking about? Who's gone? What happened?"

"It's Dylan," she cried. "He booked a flight to Nashville. He must've left overnight. He's gone, Ainsley. He's just gone."

CHAPTER THIRTY-ONE

PETER

"Hey, Dad." Dylan threw himself into my arms, patting my back with a hug that said he missed me as much as I knew he must've.

I pulled back, taking a closer look at him. "Hey, bud. I've missed you."

"Me too. I'm glad you called. When I saw Mom's number...I never expected it to be you."

"I know. I'm sure you have a lot of questions, and I understand why you haven't been answering my calls. But I was so glad to get ahold of you."

"Your calls? I...I've been trying to call you."

I swallowed. "Oh." *Ainsley.*

"Mom said you were working and didn't have service."

I nodded slowly as it began to sink in. She really had thought of everything, hadn't she? Or...*almost* everything, anyway. "Yeah. Well, I'll explain that in a minute. Right now, I want to hear about you. How was your visit with Glennon and Seth?"

"Eh, it was alright. Glad to be home, though."

Lifting his bag with one hand, I slung the other around his shoulders as we began to make our way through the airport.

"What happened to your wrist?" he asked, staring at my freshly bandaged wrist resting on his shoulder.

I pulled it back, shaking my head noncommittally. "Oh, it's nothing. How are your brother and sister?"

"Fine, I guess. Annoying as ever." He laughed. "I'm sorry we all left. Mom didn't give us a choice, you know?"

"Yeah." I was quiet for a moment. "Dylan, about that, I've got some bad news. About Mom."

He stopped. "What is it? Is it about why you had her phone? Is she okay?"

"Yeah, she is. At least, for now, anyway." I urged him forward as I caught sight of the exit doors. "Come on, we'll talk more about it in the car."

"Okay, yeah. Sure." He sounded more confident than I was sure he felt, his jaw locked tight.

A few minutes later, once we'd made it to the car, I loaded his bag in the trunk and sat down in the driver's seat. His expression was distraught, obviously imagining the worst.

"I'm not sure what your mom told you about what's going on between us..."

"She said you're separating. That you're probably going to get divorced." His eyes searched mine. "Is that true?"

I huffed out a sigh, looking down and pinching the bridge of my nose. "Unfortunately, yeah. That's what she wants."

"But you don't? Can't you just, like, talk to her? Can't you just buy her some flowers or something? It's just a stupid fight, right? There has to be a way to—"

I put a hand up to stop him. "I wish it was just a stupid fight, but your mom's got her mind made up. I..." I pressed a thumb to my lips, looking away for a beat, and then looked back at him, my mouth hanging open. "I don't really know how to tell you this. I've thought all this time about how I would tell you, but I guess I'll just come right out with it...your mom is having an affair."

He jerked his head back. "A what? Seriously?"

"She's met a man named Matt. He's young, looks like he's your age, and they've fallen for each other."

"You can't be serious. Mom wouldn't do that—"

"There are things you don't know about her, bud. It's...look, this isn't easy to tell you, but this isn't the first man this has happened with."

"What? No."

"We've always worked it out. No matter what. I've looked the other way and forgiven her time and time again. I love your mother, son. I love you guys. And I want us to be together, but...this time, she's too far gone. She won't listen to me. I can't convince her—"

"Let me talk to her. She listens to us. She can't want this—"

"Listen, there will be time for all of that, but right now, it's not safe."

"What do you mean?"

I turned away from him, starting the car. "Nothing. I shouldn't have said that. Ignore me."

"No, Dad, tell me what you meant."

"It's not my place. You're just kids. This is between the adults. It's all going to be okay. I need you to believe that. I promise you, somehow, I'm going to make sure it's okay."

"I'm not a kid, Dad. I'm practically a man now," Dylan said, his voice purposefully deeper than before. "You can trust me."

I weighed my options, drumming my fingers on the steering wheel. "Matt's...not a good guy. I'll leave it at that."

"Not a good guy? What does that mean?"

"Look, I don't know what's going on between your mother and this kid, but the reason this all came to light was because I saw a bruise on her back."

"A bruise?" He sounded horrified. "Like...like he hurt her?"

I didn't answer straight away. "She never confirmed it, but I suspected. That was when she admitted she was having the affair. She took you kids away because he was planning to meet her in Florida, but then he changed his mind—I think he was mad that you guys were with her—which is why you left in such a hurry, I'm assuming. She came home and sent you kids away so she could smooth things over with him. She must've blocked your number in my phone, or mine in yours, something. It's why I couldn't reach you. I tried to call you every day, son. I've...been worried sick."

"What the hell?" he asked under his breath. I didn't chastise him for cursing like Ainsley would've. This was life under Dad's rule. "Why would she do that? Why wouldn't she want us to talk to you?"

"I wish I had an answer. Maybe she was afraid I'd tell you the truth. I've tried so hard to keep you kids out of it. But...when I saw her yesterday, she had these...these cuts all over her face. Bruises. Like she'd been thrown into a wall. Or a floor."

"But then...you have to do something. You have to help her."

"I would if I could, but she won't let me around. She's staying at your grandmother's. Matt's there. For all I know, he's hurting them both. I...I'm at a loss, son."

"So call the police. Have them save her. She can't want this." He was on the verge of crying then, though neither of us acknowledged it.

I nodded slowly. "It's hard, sometimes, realizing your parents are...we're just human, bud. We make mistakes all the time. Bad decisions. Your mom made a really bad decision, and now, I'm not sure there's any saving her."

"You have to try!" he shouted, angry now.

Yes. Use that anger. Channel it.

"Well, there is one way, but...it's... No, it's too much. We can't. I'm sure she'll be fine. She'll come to her senses. Your mom is smart."

"What? Tell me. What's the way?"

"There are some people in this world who don't

deserve to live, Dylan. Murderers. Terrorists. People who hurt women and children."

"What are you saying?"

"Matt is going to keep hurting her unless we do something to stop it."

"What? Like...hurt him?" He waited. When I didn't respond right away, he added, "Or...or *kill* him? You can't mean that. It... That's insane."

"I know. I said it's too much. It's ridiculous. I'm just so worried about her, you know? That's why I have her phone. She brought it to me yesterday, so I have no way to contact her anymore. I guess he doesn't want her to have one. It's... It's all just happened so fast, and the police won't do anything because she says she's fine. I don't know what else to do."

"Yeah, but, I mean, there has to be a way, right? We could fight him, maybe. You and me. Two against one. Or...we could get proof. Pictures of her. We could hire a private investigator—"

"There's no more money," I said, shaking my head. "He stole everything from us. I'm working hard to keep the lights on, but he made her drain the account. And, as for fighting, he's bigger than us both. It's not worth the risk. The only way I can think of is to surprise him. Take him out." I swallowed. "It's terrible. I wish there was any other way."

"So, what are you going to do?" he asked after a moment.

"I have no idea. I can't even get inside. Maybe I'll try to break in at some point, but I don't know how long we have. I'm sorry to put all of this on you, Dylan, but it's like you said, you're almost a man now. It's time you started seeing the world for what it is. It's time you know how dangerous and evil the world can be."

He stared out the window, unusually quiet, and I wondered if I'd pushed him too hard. Finally, he looked back at me with a grim expression.

"I'll do it. I can get inside."

"No. I can't ask you to do that."

"It's our only choice, Dad. You said it yourself. We have to protect her."

I chewed my bottom lip, suppressing a smile. "Okay, then we'll have to make a plan."

CHAPTER THIRTY-TWO

AINSLEY

"Okay, listen, you just have to breathe," Mom was saying. "I'm sure he's fine. He's probably just here to see his friends."

"He's not old enough to just...do that, Mom. Not without permission or anyone knowing where he is. He stole from Glennon. He's run away. This isn't just sneaking out to see his friends."

I dialed his number, pressing the phone to my ear.

Come on.

Come on.

Come on.

Come on.

"Hey, it's Dylan. Leave me a message."

"Dylan, sweetheart, it's Mom. I need you to call me back, okay? I know you're home and...and I'm not mad, okay? I'm just really worried. We're all worried. So, please, just call me and let me know what's going on." I ended the call and crossed the room. "Do you have pictures of him anywhere?"

"There's one on the shelf in the corner," Mom said, pointing across the living room. "Why do you need one?"

"To show the police," I said, picking up the photo. "Mom, this was from ten years ago. Don't you have anything more recent?" I stared down at the photo of the five of us. Maisy was still just a baby. We looked so happy then.

"I don't, um, I don't know." She scrolled through her phone.

"You don't have anything on your phone?" Matt asked, eyeing the picture suspiciously.

"I don't have my phone. My ex-husband took it. That's why I had to use Mom's."

"Ex-husband?" he asked, obviously shocked. I'd left out that minor detail, I realized, but I had no time to care.

"Forget it. This will have to do," I said, still holding the picture.

"I think I saw a more recent photo upstairs, didn't I, Adele?" Matt asked suddenly. "In the hall."

"You did?" she asked, glancing toward the stairs.

"Can you go check? I'll stay with Ainsley. I'm worried she's going to send herself into shock." He placed a hand on my shoulder.

"I'm fine." I searched for my shoes and purse, realizing I had neither.

"You're not fine," he said as Mom hastened up the stairs. I was still looking for shoes to slip on, pacing the room as I tried to put together a plan.

"Peter must've called him on my phone. It's the only thing that makes sense. He has my phone, and now suddenly, Dylan's missing."

"Peter is your husband?" Matt asked. "The man in that photograph?"

"Yes. He's dangerous. I know I sound terrible, but I had his number blocked, so he couldn't call Dylan from his own, and there's no way he managed to figure out that it was blocked, let alone how to unblock it— *Hey, what are you doing?*"

Matt grabbed my arm, shoving me into the laundry room with a hand over my mouth. I struggled to get away from him, so sick of being manhandled by men, as my body screamed in agony. Everything hurt. Inside and out.

"*Let me go!*" I shouted, my words suppressed by the weight of his palm.

"Shut up!" he whispered, closing the door behind us gently. He flicked the light on. "There's something you should know, and there's not much time."

"There's *no* time, Matt. I've got to go to the police, my son is missing, and—"

"I've seen your husband before," he blurted out, hands at his sides.

"You-you've what?"

"I've seen him. I didn't realize it until I saw that picture." He gestured to the frame still in my hand. "But it's him."

"What are you talking about? Where have you seen him?"

He closed his eyes, bracing for the bomb he was about to drop. "Here. He's...I think he's been working with your mother."

CHAPTER THIRTY-THREE

PETER

I placed the gun in my son's hands. It would be the easiest way to kill him. From a distance. There was no need to get his hands dirty just yet.

I never wanted this life for my children, but now, I had no choice. Ainsley had taken my choices away, and I had to deal with that. This was the only way.

"Okay, safety's here." I pointed. "Keep it on until you're ready to shoot. Do you hear me?"

He nodded, eyes trained on the gun.

"Go in the front door. They'll be so happy to see you, no one will notice it. I'll sneak in through the laundry room. Keep it in your belt until you're behind him. Now, if he tries to hurt you, you have the weapon, but I don't think he will. Get behind him, point the gun, and shoot. Don't second-guess. Don't overthink. It's the only way. I'll be right there to protect you."

He was trembling, his face pale, eyes wide. He couldn't seem to wrap his fingers around the gun.

I put a hand on his shoulder, forcing him to look at me. "Dylan, I need you to promise me you can do this. I'm not going to send you in there if you can't handle it."

He met my eyes, swallowing. "I-I can handle it."

"You sure?"

"Yeah." He gripped the gun. "I'll be okay."

"After it's over, I'll take care of everything. No one will ever know. I promise you."

"No police?" he croaked.

"No police," I assured him. "Your mom would be the only one who could tell, and she's not going to want you to go to prison. You'll be saving us. Bringing us all back together."

My phone chimed with a text message from **M**.

Dylan is missing. Is he with you?

"They know you're gone," I told him.

"Mom's been calling me all morning," he admitted, looking guilty. "From Grandma's phone. I was scared to answer."

"That was smart. We don't want to give them the upper hand."

I texted my mother-in-law back quickly. **I've got him. He's safe. Let me in the side door and I'll explain.**

"Alright." I studied him, nodding affirmatively. "You ready?"

"Mhm." He didn't look ready, but he pushed the door open anyway, sliding the gun in the back of his belt like I'd shown him. He crossed the street, making his way up the walk just as I jogged across her lawn toward the side door.

He rang the doorbell, and it opened in an instant. I pressed my body to the side of the house, waiting until it shut to knock on the exterior side door that led to the laundry room.

I waited, then knocked again.

When no one answered, I twisted the knob. It was locked, as I'd expected.

Come on, Adele. Where are you?

I didn't have time to waste. I shoved my hand through the glass window, ignoring the pain that tore through my hand and turned the lock. I stepped inside the house, shutting it behind me and listening closely.

"You put us all in danger, is the point!" Ainsley was screaming.

"Now, I asked you if he was dangerous, and you said no. How was I supposed to know the truth when all you do is lie to me?" Adele argued.

"You told him where we were—"

"Mom, stop!" Dylan shouted. "This isn't Dad's fault."

"I just wanted the two of you to be together again. I wanted to help you fix your marriage. All I've ever wanted for you is what I didn't have," Adele said.

"I trusted you. I trusted you, and you betrayed me." Ainsley was furious, and with good reason. If my mother-in-law hadn't told me where to find Ainsley at the hotel and arranged for Matt to take her out long enough for me to sneak in, I might not have found her at all. She was so sure

Matt would show her how much she needed me, how lucky she was to have me. That had been a major miscalculation, but still. Having her help was a tremendous boon to my plan. She'd been on my side, even more than her daughter's. She knew what a mistake it was for Ainsley to leave me. "And you," Ainsley was saying, "sweetheart, you scared us to death. Why would you do that? Why would you run away and not tell anyone?" It sounded like she was crying.

"Why are you here, Mom?" he asked, going off script. "And what did you do to your hair? Did he make you dye it?"

No.

He was supposed to pretend everything was fine until he could get a good angle and go in for the kill.

"What?"

"Why are you leaving Dad? For him? What's he done to you?"

"No. Dylan, you've got it all wrong—"

"Do I? What happened to your face? What did he do?"

"He? Oh, sweetheart, Matt didn't do this. Matt's a friend. But, listen, honey, we have to go. Your dad could be here any minute, and—"

"He's already here," he said firmly.

"What?" she gasped.

"He brought me."

"At least he brought him back to you," Adele said. "See, he was trying to help."

Ignoring her now, Ainsley spoke directly to our son.

"Dylan, there are some things you need to know about your father, and—"

"There's a car outside," Matt confirmed.

"We don't need you to tell her what I already told her, asshole," Dylan shouted, his voice erratic. He was losing control. Getting too emotional. He wasn't ready for this.

"Sorry," Matt mumbled. "I was just trying to—"

"Dylan! No!" Ainsley shouted, her voice echoing through the halls. The crack of a gunshot rang out. I smiled as I heard a thud.

A body had fallen to the floor.

His body.

I stepped out of my hiding place, taking in the scene: Matt was slumped in the corner against the wall; Adele was on the stairs, her eyes wide with the horror of what had happened; Ainsley stood in the center of the room, a hand over her agape mouth; Dylan was pale-faced and quivering, the gun dangling in his hand at his side.

"What did you do?" Ainsley asked in horror, crossing the room to examine Matt.

"I'm sorry... I had to..." He couldn't seem to form words. It was time for me to interject.

"Attaboy," I said, approaching him from behind and placing a hand on his shoulder.

"Peter?" Ainsley stood, her back slamming into the wall. She shot a glance at Dylan, then leered at me. "You did this? You...you had him kill an innocent person? Why? Why would you do this? To get back at me?"

"Of course, he didn't," Adele argued, looking at me with disbelief. "Tell her you didn't, Peter."

"He's hardly innocent," I said, gesturing toward her face. "You can give up the act. I told him everything. He knows Matt's the one who did that to you."

"You're...you're insane. Delusion—"

At her feet, Matt groaned, his body shuddering as he released an exasperated breath.

"He's not dead." Ainsley fell to the ground, a hand over the wound on his shoulder.

"You know what you have to do," I told Dylan, lowering my mouth to his ear.

"Dylan, sweetheart, don't listen to him. Just...bring the gun to me," Ainsley urged. "Please. Please, son. Bring it to me. You're confused. You don't want to hurt anyone. I know that."

"He's protecting you, Ainsley," I argued. "Stop lying."

"Dad, I'm scared—" His voice quivered.

"Sweetheart, please," Ainsley begged, one hand on Matt's shoulder and the other—bloody and shaking—outstretched for Dylan. "Please come to me."

"You have to do it, Dylan. You have to kill him. It's the only way she'll ever be safe. It's the only way she'll ever stay with us."

"What is he talking about, Ainsley?" Adele asked.

"Is that what this is about?" Ainsley shouted, a new sort of rage filling her. Her face was pink, her entire body pulsing with electricity as she moved toward me in a flash. "You've turned our son into a murderer to punish me?"

I spun, using Dylan as a shield between us. "If she tries to hurt us, you'll have to kill her, too."

"What?" Dylan was crying then—his face coated in snot and tears.

"Don't listen to him, Dylan. He's a bad man. Your father is a bad, bad man. He's a murderer. I've tried so hard to protect you kids from all that he's done, and now he wants you to kill me, too. Matt is innocent." She lowered her face to meet his eyes. "Do you hear me?"

"Don't listen to her," I warned him.

"Matt did nothing wrong. He is a friend. A friend who has been really kind to me. These marks on my face, your father made those. Not Matt. Your father has been working behind my back with your grandmother, trying to set this all up."

"Ainsley, I didn't know!" Adele cried.

Ainsley didn't budge, staring only at me. "I should've known she was the one telling you how to find me."

"She wants us to be together," I said simply. "She knows how good I am for you."

"Oh, for heaven's sake, stop this, both of you," Adele cried, fanning herself as if she were going to pass out.

Ainsley looked down at the blood on her hands, scoffing and taking a step forward. "How good you are for me, Peter? Really?"

"Ainsley, we are good together. Your parents want us to be together. The kids want us to be together."

"The kids don't know the truth about you—"

"Or you—" I warned. Two could play that game.

Ainsley turned her focus back to our son. "Dylan, please, baby. Please give me the gun."

"If you give it to her, she'll shoot us both. She'd do anything to save him."

She shook her head, her forehead creased with concern. "You know I wouldn't do that, don't you? You know I'd never hurt you. Not in a million years, Dylan. I love you. I love your brother and your sister. Think about them, okay? Get out of your head about what your dad's told you, and think about what you know is real. I know this is really scary, but there are things you know, right? You know I'd never hurt you. You know that in your gut." She pressed a hand to her stomach. "You have to."

Behind us, Matt groaned again. "Ains..." he whispered, no strength in his words.

Just die already, tough guy.

She took another step toward me, her eyes locked with mine. "He'll never forgive you, Peter. He'll never forgive you when he learns the truth. You can't take this back. You can't undo it. Even if you kill Matt, even if you kill me, someday, they'll know the truth about who you are and what you've done. And on that day, their hatred for you will be all they'll know. You're going to let him do something that can't be undone, something that will forever change him, for your own sake. Because this isn't for Dylan. It's for you."

"No. That's not true. I'm doing what I have to do to protect this family."

"How is any of this protecting this family? You're hurting this family!"

Matt groaned, and I reached for Dylan's arms, pulling the gun into position. "Pull the trigger," I ordered. "Kill him."

"Dylan, don't listen to him." Ainsley stepped in front of Matt, her hands up.

"You may not care enough to protect yourself," I snarled at her through gritted teeth, "but you'd do anything to protect your kids. So choose now, Ainsley... Who will you put over your son? If Matt dies, Dylan has just killed someone. How far will you go to protect that secret? Stay with me and protect him or...don't."

"What?" Dylan whimpered, trying to step away from me. I wrapped my arms around him tighter, the gun still in his hand.

"You wouldn't," she snarled.

"I think you've seen just how far I'll go to keep you. So, tell me, who's more important? You or him?"

"Dad," Dylan cried, looking at me over his shoulder with such complete heartbreak it was almost enough to make me stop. Almost.

"Him." She sobbed, her voice powerless. "Him. Of course it's him. I will do whatever you want. Just stop." Her hands were up. "I'll come home. I'll do whatever you want, just please don't make him do this."

"Stop!" Dylan shouted, struggling to free himself. "Both of you, just stop!" He shoved his head back, head-butting me.

I pulled back, covering my lip. I could already taste

the blood. "Why the hell would you do that? I thought you were with me!"

"He doesn't want to do this, you monster!" Ainsley said, through tears of her own.

She reached for him, and he took a step toward her, holding out the gun.

"I'm so sorry, Mom," he cried, falling into her arms.

She held him tight, patting his back gently and shushing in his ear. "It's okay, baby. It's all going to be okay."

I stepped toward her and she lifted the gun, pushing Dylan behind her.

Fuck.

"Call 9-1-1," she ordered him. "Find Matt's phone and call 9-1-1."

He darted across the room, doing as she said and searching in his pockets for the phone. I backed away, hands up.

"You don't want to do this, Dylan. You'll go to jail. You pulled that trigger, not me."

Ainsley stepped between us, so I could no longer see him. "He's not dead. No one's going to jail. No one except you."

"You really think it'll be that easy?" I asked. "Your word against mine. How do you know Adele won't side with me? She usually does." I cast a glance at the stairs, not entirely sure my mother-in-law hadn't passed out. "How do you know I won't start spilling secrets in jail and make sure you join me?"

"What's he talking about?" Dylan asked.

"Call the police and find out." I shrugged.

"Mom?" he asked. Wimp that he was.

"I could kill you, you know. It would be self-defense," she snarled, pressing the gun into my chest.

Dylan stood, moving toward her. Maybe he'd grown a backbone after all. "Please don't, Mom. Please just let him go."

She glanced over her shoulder at him. "Dylan, if I let him go, he'll never stop coming for us. We'll never be safe. I have to protect you. You and your brother and sister. From all monsters—under the bed and inside the house." She turned back, her jaw tight, but he put his hand on her arm.

"Please. For me. Please don't kill him. Just let him go. Just...let's go get Maisy and Riley. Let's just go." When he looked at me, his eyes were cold and dead. Emotionless. It was like looking at a stranger.

He hated me.

Well, join the club, kid.

"Please, I'm sorry. I'm so sorry. But I can't lose you, too." He sobbed against her shoulder. "I can't lose you, too."

She dropped the gun to her side, pulling him into a hug, and stared at me over his shoulder. "Go, Peter. Go and never come back. This is the last warning I'll ever give you."

"Neither of you mean this. You're...angry and hurt, but..."

"*Go, Peter.*" She'd already turned away from me, leading Dylan back over to where Matt lay. Dylan helped her apply pressure in what felt like a scene from my worst nightmare, as they worked to save a man that wasn't me. A man that would ruin my whole life. A man that had taken what was mine.

I stood there for several seconds, watching it unfold, before turning and walking away. I didn't run—didn't need to. They weren't watching and they didn't care.

After everything I'd done to protect my family, everything I'd done to save my marriage, they'd all given up on me.

People are so disappointing.

CHAPTER THIRTY-FOUR

AINSLEY

ONE YEAR LATER

"Well, what do you think of the place?" I asked the kids, staring around the foyer of our new home.

"It's really nice, Momma," Maisy said. "Can I pick my room?"

"Of course. You'd better, in fact, before Aunt Glennon and Uncle Seth get here to pick out theirs."

"Race ya," Riley said, elbowing her playfully before the two dashed across the room and up the stairs.

Dylan stayed behind, remaining beside me, and when we were alone, he cleared his throat. "This is nice. I think Boulder could be good for us."

"I think so, too. New scenery. New memories to make."

"Yeah, it's cool." He was quiet for a second, looking around. "Is Matt going to move in, too?"

I cocked my head to the side. "Would you be cool with it if he did?"

He thought about it for a moment, then said, "I think so. Yeah."

"Good to know. We haven't made any plans for that. Right now, he's going to stay at his apartment here, and we'll take things slow."

"He moved across the country for you, Mom. I wouldn't exactly call that slow."

I patted his shoulder. "You kids are my top priority, okay? Now that you're settled and enrolled in school, and we're finally out of that apartment, we'll see what happens. But I'm enjoying time with just you guys. I'm not looking to change that anytime soon."

"Okay. Cool." He nodded. "Hey, uh, they're...they're doing okay." He jutted his head toward the stairs. "I check in with them sometimes, just in case, and they miss him, but they're okay. We're all okay."

I pressed my lips together, tears stinging my eyes. "Yeah?"

"Yeah."

"What did I ever do to deserve a kid like you?" I asked, pulling him in and kissing the top of his head. He wrapped one arm around me in a halfhearted hug.

"Just lucky, I guess." When he pulled away, he pointed toward the stairs. "I'm going to go see if there are any rooms left that haven't been claimed for libraries and gaming lounges. Love ya."

"I love you too, kiddo."

As he bounded up the stairs, Glennon appeared in

the doorway. "Knock knock." When she saw me, she paused, tilting her head to the side with concern. "Everything okay?"

"More than okay." I slipped my arm around her waist, tears stinging my eyes. "Thank you for...for everything, Glennon."

"You know I've got your back, babe. This family may be a little dysfunctional—"

"I prefer to think of it as modern."

She laughed. "*Modern* then, it may be a little modern, but we'll make it work. We'll be the best damn family this world has ever seen."

Tears fell freely then. There was so much I still couldn't say, still couldn't tell her, but somehow, as she wrapped me in a hug, she seemed to understand. "You're free," she whispered. "You're free, love." She pulled back, brushing tears from my eyes and pointing around the room. "Your kids are free and safe, and *you* did that." She poked her finger into my chest. "You. Never forget it."

"I won't."

"I'll be there to remind you if you do." She hugged me again.

A knock on the door sounded, and I dusted my cheeks, sniffling. "Come in."

Matt walked into the room, a large box in his hands. "Where do you want this?"

"Oh, just anywhere you can find a spot."

He placed the box down and walked toward me, kissing my temple. "Hi, beautiful." He tilted his head to the side. "Everything okay?"

"Just dust," I told him, rubbing my palms over my eyes.

"Lots of dust," Glennon agreed with a dry laugh, wiping tears of her own.

I wrapped one arm around Matt and one around Glennon, my heart so full of happiness, peace, and safety I was sure it was going to explode.

They hugged me back, standing perfectly still, waiting on me to be ready to let them go.

The truth was, I wasn't sure I'd ever be ready. We were coming up on the anniversary of the day my life imploded, and they expected it to be hard. In truth, I expected it to be hard. But it was the easiest thing I'd ever done.

Living without Peter, building a life entirely my own, was the best thing I'd ever done for myself, for my kids, for my friends. I'd dropped the weight of the family that was supposed to matter—my nonexistent father, backstabbing mother, and monster of a husband—and fully embraced the family I built. Peter may have been the architect, but my designs were a pretty amazing thing to behold. Our life now was a beautiful, peaceful thing.

I'd never known peace like it.

No more voices in my head telling me I wasn't good enough. Not perfect enough. No more fears that if I lost Peter, I'd lose everything. Now I knew what I wish I'd known then—I didn't need him. Didn't need anyone, except my kids.

There was a freedom that came with that. That came

with burning it all down and rebuilding. Handpicking every part of your life, every person in your life.

"Did I hear Aunt Glennon?" Maisy cried from upstairs, sounding excited.

"That's my cue," she said, dashing away from us.

Matt kissed me again, this time on my lips. "Want to help me bring in the rest of the boxes?"

"It's all I've ever dreamed of." I chuckled. "I'll be right there. I just have to take care of something first."

He rubbed a finger over my cheek, then turned away and made his way out the door. I never thought anyone like Matt could make me happy. Someone so young, so unlike Peter. But his youth brought with it a sense of hope I'd never experienced. A kindness. An attentiveness. Matt treated me as if I was the sun and he was just glad to be in my orbit. The kids had taken a while to warm up to him, but they had. Glennon adored him. He was everything I needed in a package I'd never have chosen.

I mused over how perfectly things had worked out as I sifted through boxes, searching for one in particular that was labeled...

Collectibles—Ainsley

There it was.

I picked up the box and carried it up the stairs, passing Maisy and Glennon in one room as they deliberated over the perfect place to hang a photo, and Riley in the next room, already flopped down in a beanbag chair with a bag of potato chips. His brother sat next to him, laughing about something I hadn't heard. I moved forward, finding the room that would be mine.

It felt strange. I'd be able to choose the side of the bed I wanted. The entire closet could be mine. I could choose every bit of the decor. There was no one around to argue with anymore.

And there never would be again.

I shut the door behind me, turning the lock, and placed the box on the floor. The old owners of our home had had a floor safe installed, where they'd kept their gun close to their bed. When the realtor had shown it to me, I'd known instantly this was the one.

I reached into the box and retrieved the old black bag, unzipping it and staring inside. It was empty now, all of Peter's treasures long gone, but I now understood the appeal.

The treasures remind us they were real.

Inside of the bag, there was an envelope.

I pulled it out, checking over my shoulder once to be sure I wasn't being watched. Then, I turned the envelope over and, with a huff of relieved breath, the kind of breath only freedom could bring, I let the tuft of brown hair fall into my palm.

Now, there really were no more secrets.

CHAPTER THIRTY-FIVE

AINSLEY

SIX MONTHS EARLIER

I sat outside the corporate office of my old job with butterflies in my belly. I wasn't sure why I was so nervous. I had this under control. Tina said Burt wanted to talk to me about a new position that was opening up now that I was settled into our new apartment. When they'd initially refused to transfer me, I'd taken a job as a secretary at a legal firm, anything to make sure I had income and insurance again, but I couldn't deny that I missed doing what I loved. What I was good at.

If they'd offer me a job again, I'd take it in a heartbeat.

I'd flown back to Nashville to talk to him in person, as he wanted to make absolutely sure the person heading up their newest branch was a great fit, according to Tina.

I crossed the street cautiously, a lump in my throat.

I'd never been so nervous.

"Good morning," the receptionist greeted me from behind thick-framed glasses. "Can I help you?"

"I'm here for a meeting with Burt Stover. I'm Ainsley Greenburg."

"Okay, just a minute." He raised the phone to his ear, dialing two digits. "Mr. Stover, I have a Ms. Greenburg here to see you. Excellent. I'll send her up." He hung up the phone and gestured toward the elevators to my left. "You'll take these elevators to the third floor and turn to your right. You'll see the HR waiting area at the end of the hall."

"Thank you," I said, patting the counter and making my way toward the elevator. Once the doors had shut, I inhaled, releasing the breath slowly. It was all going to be okay.

Following his instructions, I turned right, spying a waiting area behind a glass wall. I walked into the room, knocking cautiously. A plump woman with short blonde hair grinned at me.

"You're Mrs. Greenburg?"

"Ms.," I corrected. "And yes."

"Mr. Stover is expecting you. You can go straight back. His office is the last one on your left." She pointed down a hallway to our right. "Would you like a bottle of water or anything?"

"I'm okay. Thank you." I clasped my hands together, my heels clicking on the tile floor as I made my way down the dark hall. His name was printed in black on the glass of the door and, when I reached it, I knocked.

"Come in." The voice sent chills down my spine. I hesitated.

Breathe. You can do this.

I pushed the door open, my body going rigid as I saw the man waiting for me.

"Peter?"

"No," he said, standing up, both hands on the desk in front of him. "Burt Stover."

"H-how?" A block of ice settled in my core.

"Sit down." He pointed to the seat in front of his desk.

"Not a chance."

"Did you meet Beth out there?" He nodded toward the door. "Nice old lady. Beat breast cancer twice. She has twelve grandkids. Can you imagine? Twelve." He twisted his lips. "Be a shame if she didn't get to see those grandkids this Christmas, wouldn't it?"

A wave of panic washed over me, and I sat. "What do you want, Peter? How are you here?"

"Jim left quite a few useful things behind, didn't he? Sedatives, fake identities..."

"You impersonated Burt Stover?"

"I *created* Burt Stover," he said. "Way back when I needed a way to contact you the first time. When I thought you'd be harder to find. I thought I'd keep him in my pocket, just in case. Turns out, it was a good plan because I was going to lose my job and need a replacement anyway."

"What do you want, Peter?"

He took a seat on the desktop in front of me. "*You.*

Don't you see that? I want *you*. I'm never going to stop coming after you. I'm never going to stop searching. If you won't be with me, you sure as hell don't get to go off and live a perfect little life as if I don't exist." He moved behind my chair, his voice in my ear. "I'll be the noise you think you heard in the shower." He bounced to the other side. "I'll be the bump in the night." A chill ran down my neck. "The person you swore you saw in a dimly lit parking garage. You'll never escape me. Never be rid of me. Never—"

I rammed the stun gun into his neck and engaged it, stopping his words. He fell forward on top of me, quivering with the pulse of it, and I pushed up out of the seat, holding it out in front of him.

"Do you really think I expected any less? I know you, Peter. I know that you're relentless. I've been waiting for you. Trying to anticipate when you'd strike. You're never quite as smart as you think you are. The day Tina told me about Burt Stover, I looked him up. Company pictures are public info. I saw who you were. It's why I stopped trying to get the job. I knew what you were up to, knew you'd use it to try and catch me. I never thought it would take this long, though. Patience was never your strong suit."

"We're...all...having to *adapt*, aren't we?" he asked, finding his voice again. He stretched his arms, popping his neck. "What's your plan here, Ainsley? What can you possibly do to me right now?"

"Right now? Nothing. But Beth goes to lunch at twelve thirty. I'm the only interview for this position, so no one will be on this floor while she's gone, which means I can get you to the elevator and downstairs in one of the empty conference rooms. Then, I just have to wait until Marcus takes a bathroom—*actually social media*—break, and I can get you outside. I'm assuming you shut off all the cameras today, planning to do the same thing to me." I pursed my lips, watching the rage flash through his eyes in confirmation. "You should've just stayed away, Peter. Really, you should've. But I told you if I ever saw you again, it would be for the last time, and I meant it."

He lunged at me, shoving me into the desk, and I pulled the syringe of sedative out—the last one I had.

How fitting.

I bit the lid off as he fought to swipe it from my hands. I was too fast. I wrapped my legs around his waist with every ounce of strength I had to keep him from moving and shoved the needle into his side.

"You...bitch..." he mumbled, trying and failing to fight. The dose was strong, it would work fast and last a long time, which was what I needed.

I grinned at him, my chest swelling with pride as I shoved him to the ground. He panted, trying yet failing to get up. It was over. Finally, it was all going to be over. I leaned down, staring into his eyes as they went hazy.

Seconds before he closed them for what would be the final time, I whispered, "Sorry, honey. This *bitch* just won."

ENJOYED THE ATONEMENT?

If you enjoyed this story, please consider leaving me a quick review. It doesn't have to be long—just a few words will do. Who knows? Your review might be the thing that encourages a future reader to take a chance on my work!

To leave a review, please visit:

mybook.to/theatonement

Let everyone know how much you loved
The Atonement on Goodreads:
https://bit.ly/3yZkhOn

DON'T MISS THE NEXT PSYCHOLOGICAL THRILLER FROM KIERSTEN MODGLIN

Thank you so much for reading this story. I'd love to invite you to sign up for my mailing list and text alerts so we can be sure you don't miss my next release.

Sign up for my mailing list here:
kierstenmodglinauthor.com/nlsignup

Sign up for my text alerts here:
kierstenmodglinauthor.com/textalerts

ACKNOWLEDGMENTS

First and foremost, to my phenomenal husband and amazing little girl—I love you both more than you will ever know. Thank you for believing in me, cheering me on, traveling with me, taking leaps with me, and for being there every step of the way. I couldn't do this without you two.

To my bestie, Emerald O'Brien—thank you for always knowing what to say or what question to ask. Thank you for talking me through this series as I created it, for encouraging me to write the second, and eventually the third book when I wasn't sure, and for being the absolute best friend anyone could ask for. Love you, friend.

To my immensely talented editor, Sarah West—thank you for always seeing the vision and helping me to perfect it.

To the proofreading team at My Brother's Editor—thank you for giving my stories their final polish.

To my loyal readers (AKA the #KMod Squad)—I could never thank you enough for making my wildest dreams come true. For every email, social media post, review, recommendation to your friends, bookstore order, KU download, and so much more. You guys keep me going on my worst day. I'm so grateful for your support, encouragement, and belief in me. Thank you for loving Peter and Ainsley from the start and for begging for more! This trilogy exists because of you.

To my book club—Sara, both Erins, June, Heather, Dee, and Rhonda—thank you for being the ones I can talk to about anything and everything, and the ones who make me laugh no matter what. I'm so thankful for our amazing group and for your friendship. Love you, girls.

To my agent, Carly Watters, thank you for believing in me and my stories, and for helping to get them in front of new readers.

Last but certainly not least, to you—thank you for purchasing this book and supporting my art. Growing up, I dreamed that someday someone would pick up a book with my name on the cover, crack it open, and discover a world entirely of my own creation. With this purchase, you made my dream come true. I'm so very grateful for you. Whether this is your first KMod book or your 33rd, I hope it was everything you hoped for and nothing like you expected.

ABOUT THE AUTHOR

KIERSTEN MODGLIN is an Amazon Top 10 bestselling author of psychological thrillers and a member of International Thriller Writers, Novelists, Inc., and the Alliance of Independent Authors. Kiersten is a KDP Select All-Star and a recipient of *ThrillerFix*'s Best Psychological Thriller Award and *Suspense Magazine*'s Best Book of 2021 Award. She grew up in rural western Kentucky and later relocated to Nashville, Tennessee, where she now lives with her husband, daughter, and their two Boston terriers: Cedric and Georgie. Kiersten's work is currently being translated into multiple languages and readers across the world refer to her as 'The Queen of Twists.' A Netflix addict, Shonda Rhimes superfan, psychology fanatic, and *indoor* enthusiast, Kiersten enjoys rainy days spent with her nose in a book.

Sign up for Kiersten's newsletter here:
kierstenmodglinauthor.com/nlsignup

Sign up for text alerts from Kiersten here:
kierstenmodglinauthor.com/textalerts

kierstenmodglinauthor.com
www.facebook.com/kierstenmodglinauthor
www.facebook.com/groups/kmodsquad
www.twitter.com/kmodglinauthor
www.instagram.com/kierstenmodglinauthor
www.tiktok.com/@kierstenmodglinauthor
www.goodreads.com/kierstenmodglinauthor
www.bookbub.com/authors/kiersten-modglin
www.amazon.com/author/kierstenmodglin

ALSO BY KIERSTEN MODGLIN

STANDALONE NOVELS

Missing Daughter

The Reunion

Tell Me the Truth

The Dinner Guests

ARRANGEMENT NOVELS

The Arrangement (Book 1)

The Amendment (Book 2)

THE MESSES SERIES

The Cleaner (The Messes, #1)

The Healer (The Messes, #2)

The Liar (The Messes, #3)

The Prisoner (The Messes, #4)

NOVELLAS

The Long Route: A Lover's Landing Novella

The Stranger in the Woods: A Crimson Falls Novella

THE LOCKE INDUSTRIES SERIES

The Nanny's Secret

Made in the USA
Monee, IL
14 June 2024